VILLA'S RIFLES

VILLA'S RIFLES

Lewis B. Patten

Chivers Press • G.K. Hall & Co.
Bath, Avon, England • Thorndike, Maine USA

This Large Print edition is published by Chivers Press, England, and by G.K. Hall & Co., USA.

Published in 1995 in the U.K. by arrangement with Doubleday (UK) Limited.

Published in 1994 in the U.S. by arrangement with the Golden West Literary Agency.

U.K. Hardcover ISBN 0–7451–2378–3 (Chivers Large Print)
U.S. Softcover   ISBN 0–8161–7424–5 (Nightingale Series Edition)

The text of this Large Print edition is unabridged.
Other aspects of the book may vary from the original edition.

Set in 16pt. New Times Roman.

Printed in the U.K. on acid-free paper.

British Library Cataloguing in Publication Data available

Library of Congress Cataloging-in-Publication Data

Patten, Lewis B.
    Villa's rifles / Lewis B. Patten.
        p.   cm.
    ISBN 0–8161–7424–5 (alk. paper : lg. print)
    1. Large type books.   I. Title.
[PS3566.A79V55   1994]
813′.54—dc20
                                                                94–20140

CHAPTER ONE

In sight of the small adobe ranch house, Ezra Pew halted his five men and sat his horse for several moments staring down at it.

The sun was down but the stain it had cast upon the clouds above the western horizon still provided ample light.

Pew was a big man, over six feet tall, broad of shoulder and deep of chest. He weighed two hundred and twenty pounds and the only fat visible on him was the bulge at his middle. He was fully bearded and there was gray both in his beard and in his hair. Above his beard his nose was flattened and red, lined with blue veins. His eyes were close-set and grayish-blue. His character showed more in those close-set eyes than in anything else. His face, hidden by the beard, usually revealed little expression. But the eyes were always visible and they could not conceal the cold viciousness of the man. He was a killer who killed with as little thought as he would have given to stepping on a bug. He was known and wanted in half a dozen states for crimes ranging from murder and rape to bank robbery.

Slightly behind him, spread out so that they could also see, were his men. Karl Hines was second in command. Younger than Pew, he was muscular, equally dirty, and wearing a four-day growth of whiskers on his face. There was a glow in Hines's greenish eyes because he knew the chances were good that there was a woman down there in that adobe house.

Les Chisum was skinny and short, a man whose physical inadequacy against other men had prompted him to become highly proficient with the gun he wore. Pew had once said that Chisum reminded him of a sidewinder, small but deadly, one no sane man would provoke.

Al Brunner sat his saddle like a huge, sagging lump of clay. He too wore a full beard but it couldn't hide the thick folds of flesh at his jowls and neck. He was even filthier than the others if that was possible. He had probably killed as many or more men than any of the others had, but because he was fat and slow, he did it unexpectedly at short range simply by ramming a derringer against his victim's body and firing.

Beside him sat his brother Joe, younger, less fat but equally stocky of build.

Del Quigley was the last of the outlaw band. He was slender and brown-eyed with a ready smile and white, even teeth that seemed even whiter beneath the sweeping, tawny mustache he always wore. Quigley was a ladies' man and he too was thinking that there probably was a woman in the ranch house down below. Fussier than Hines, he hoped she would be a pretty one, and he knew if she was, he would probably have to fight Hines over her. Slight he

2

might be, but he wasn't afraid of Hines or of anybody else. It was because of this total lack of fear that the others had such a healthy respect for him. They let him strictly alone.

The sun glow began to fade from the piled-up, puffy clouds. Pew waited until they had all turned gray and then he touched his horse's sides with his spurs and the animal moved on down the slope at a steady walk.

Lamplight winked from the kitchen window of the house. A Mexican came from the adobe barn, carrying a pail of milk. He went into the house and the door closed again. A dog began to bark as the six rode into the yard.

Inside the house, Lily MacDonald looked at Heraldo Garcia, who had just come in with the milk. Garcia, along with Pedro Ramirez, helped her run the ranch left by her husband, who had been killed when a horse had fallen on him about ten months before.

'What's the dog barking at?'

He shrugged unconcernedly as he put the milk down on a long table beside the stove. Lily, with only part of her mind on the dog's now frantic barking, crossed the room to strain the milk. Garcia picked up a pan and headed toward the door to wash at the pump outside.

It opened before he could reach it. At the same time the dog in the yard yelped and then began to whine as if in pain.

The man who entered was huge and powerful, with the coldest pair of eyes Lily had

3

ever seen. She asked angrily, 'Don't you ever knock?'

He didn't bother to answer her. Five other men crowded in behind him. Their rancid smell was almost overpowering. Lily's five-year-old son, Jimmy, ran past them out the door to see what was wrong with the dog. Lily heard the dog yelp once more with pain, and immediately afterward heard Jimmy cry out as the dog apparently snapped at him.

Angry, she left the milk pail and tried to get to the door. Grinning, Karl Hines barred her way. She tried to go around him but he caught her around the waist and pulled her up close to him. 'The dog ain't hurt bad an' neither is the boy. You stay here, missus. You're a pretty one, an' that's for sure.'

She struggled to be free. Across the room, Garcia pushed himself away from the wall. He didn't carry a gun, but there was a loaded rifle hanging from two pegs on the wall and he reached for it.

He never touched it. Pew fired and Garcia, with a spot of blood showing on the back of his shirt, slid to the floor without a sound. Pew held the gun a moment, pointing it at Ramirez. Then he said, 'Joe, get that goddam gun.'

Joe Brunner crossed the room, got the rifle and unloaded it. Pew said, 'Smash it.'

Joe Brunner smashed it against the fireplace.

Lily was staring with pure horror at the motionless body of Garcia, lying slumped on the floor. She felt Karl Hines's hand exploring her body and began to struggle frantically. Pew said irritably, 'God damn it Hines, let her go! Women ain't what we came here for!'

'Maybe not,' Hines growled, 'but she's too damn pretty to pass up.'

'Later then. Right now let her go.'

Hines still did not obey. Not until Del Quigley softly said, 'Do what Ezra said, Karl. Let her go.'

Hines turned his head. 'Someday I'm going to blow your goddam head off.'

Quigley grinned. 'Any time you want to try it, go ahead.'

Pew said irritably, 'Shut up, both of you!'

Lily MacDonald was white with shock, her eyes riveted on the still form of Garcia crumpled on the floor. When Hines released her, she ran to him and dropped to her knees beside him. She groped frantically for his wrist to see if he was still alive. Ramirez started toward her but Pew said harshly, 'Stay put, or you'll get the same thing he did.'

Ramirez froze. Lily looked up at him, her face now streaked with tears. 'He's dead,' she said unbelievingly.

Outside the house, she could hear Jimmy crying. As if she were in a daze, she got up, crossed the room, and went out the door. Hines reached for her as she went past him, but dropped his hand when Pew said irritably, 'Damn it, I said let her alone!'

5

Hines seemed not to resent the rebuke. Lily disappeared through the door.

*   *   *

She was in a state of shock as she fled through the door and headed for Jimmy, crouched crying beside the dog, who lay whimpering on his side. Her mind could not yet comprehend fully that Heraldo Garcia was dead. Nor that the six terrifying characters had taken possession of her house. She could feel her body begin trembling, could feel the onslaught of hysteria, and stopped for an instant, clenching her fists, telling herself that she was not going to break down and get hysterical. It would solve nothing. It might make things worse.

What did they want, she asked herself. Why had they come to this poor and isolated place? She had no money except for the few dollars kept in a lard can on the kitchen shelf. There were no horses here, save for the buggy horse she kept in the corral and the two used today by Garcia and Ramirez. What cattle she had were widely scattered. What then, did they want?

Only one logical answer came to her mind. They were fleeing from the law. They wanted food and a place to rest for the night. They would be gone in the morning, leaving Garcia dead behind them because he had tried to protect her. At the remembrance of the way

Hines had smelled, of the way his hands had felt on her, she shuddered and a cold chill ran along her spine.

She reached her five-year-old son. He was on his knees beside the shaggy little dog they called Spot. One of his hands was up, the knuckles in his mouth and she knew Spot had bitten him.

She knelt beside her son. 'He's not hurt bad, Jimmy. He'll be all right.'

'I just touched him and he bit me. He must be hurt awful bad for him to do that.'

Lily said, 'One of them kicked him. Maybe he's got a broken rib. But it will heal.'

It was dark. The only light was that from the stars and the square lamplight cast on the ground by the open door. She had the sudden awful feeling that when the six men left this place, nothing would remain alive. Not even Jimmy or the dog.

She whispered, 'You know that cave you've got down in the riverbank?'

'Uh huh.'

'How'd you like to spend the night down there?'

Before he had time to answer, Pew came to the door of the house. 'Bring that kid and come on in.'

It was too late to get Jimmy away. Maybe later, she thought. She took Jimmy's hand, pulled him to his feet, and led him toward the house. The dog tried to get up and follow, but

7

yelped with pain and fell back, whining.

Jimmy pulled against her grasp, trying to return to the dog. But she kept a firm grip on him, almost dragging him into the house. She had seen what happened when the men were openly defied.

She went inside and Pew closed the door. Once inside she looked at Jimmy's hand. The bite was superficial but because she wanted something to do, she took him to the stove, moistened a dish towel with water from the teakettle, and washed it off.

Finished, she turned and looked at Pew. 'Why are you here? What do you want from us?'

'Don't worry about it, missus.'

'How long...?'

'We'll be gone in a day or two.'

She looked into those cold, merciless eyes and, even more than before, she was certain that when they finally did leave, no one here would remain alive.

Coldness crept through her body. Pew said, 'We're hungry. Fix us something to eat.'

She nodded wordlessly. Jimmy was staring at Garcia's body across the room. Pew caught the direction of his glance and said to Brunner, 'You and your brother get him out of here. Put him in the barn and cover him over with something.'

The pair moved to obey. They disappeared out the door, carrying Garcia's body. Jimmy asked in a barely audible voice, 'Is he dead?'

Living on a ranch, death was no stranger to Jimmy, even at the tender age of five. Lily nodded. 'Yes, Jimmy, he's dead.'

Del Quigley was staring closely at Lily's face. 'You always lived here, missus? Seems like I've seen you someplace before. Long time ago, though. Long time ago.'

Lily shook her head, without bothering to reply. She got out a couple of cast-iron skillets, put lard in both, and set them on the back of the stove. She had a couple of days' supply of potatoes in the house and she began peeling them.

The outlaws found chairs and made themselves comfortable. Some of them lighted pipes. Quigley continued to watch Lily's face. So did Hines. Quigley's stares worried her. Hines's terrified her.

She thought that if they were fleeing the law, they'd stay the night and then be gone. But their leader had said a couple of days. That had to mean something else.

She thought of Sam Chance, sheriff of Cruces County, who usually got out here to see her at least once a week. She hoped he didn't come tonight, or tomorrow. He'd only get himself killed the way Garcia had. He wouldn't stand by while one of these filthy outlaws pawed her.

Recalling that Quigley had thought he recognized her, there was guilt in her suddenly

9

as she thought of Sam. She hadn't been completely honest with him the way she had with her husband. She hadn't thought it necessary. In six years a person ought to be able to live down the past.

But if Quigley had recognized her, someone else might also recognize her, sometime, someplace.

Next time she saw Sam, she'd tell him the truth. Maybe doing so would mean losing him, but maybe it would not.

With only faint bitterness, she wondered how long it took a person to live down the past. Maybe a person never completely lived it down.

CHAPTER TWO

Sam Chance closed up the office at five. No one was in jail so there was no reason he couldn't leave. It was a long ways out to Lily MacDonald's place, but he didn't often consider that. Seeing her was worth the long ride out and the equally long ride back.

Sam Chance was thirty-five. He had been sheriff of Cruces County for five years now, and would come up for re-election next year. Whether he ran for the office again depended on several things. If he married Lily, he couldn't live out there and hold the sheriff's job as well. She'd either have to sell the ranch or he'd have to give up the sheriff's job and move out there with her.

He walked down the street to the livery stable, went in and got his horse. He led him up front and was saddling him as Dave Sorensen came out of the tackroom. Sorensen grinned at him. 'Going out to the widow's place?'

Sam nodded.

'When you going to marry her? Or ain't you asked her yet?'

'I've asked her. She wants to wait until her husband's been dead a year.'

'That's only a couple of months away.'

Sam nodded. He didn't mind discussing Lily with Dave. Dave was a friend and his interest was a friendly one.

'She's a fine-lookin' woman. You could sure do worse.'

Sam nodded. He finished saddling the horse and swung to his back. 'If anybody asks about me, I'll be back late tonight.' It was more than a dozen miles out to Lily MacDonald's place. Even pushing the horse, that was a two-hour ride. And two hours back, or three.

He rode down the wooden ramp to the street and headed toward the bridge at the lower end of town. He was looking forward to seeing Lily and he was wishing, as he had many times in the last few months, that she wasn't so stubborn about remarrying before her husband had been dead a year. He didn't want

11

to wait. It was hard leaving her at night when he wanted her so much. He always spent the ride back to town thinking about what it would be like if he'd been able to stay.

He held his horse to a steady trot. The sun sank toward the horizon and finally dropped behind it. For a little while it stained the clouds a brilliant orange, but that too faded, leaving the land gray and colorless.

A feeling of uneasiness came suddenly to Sam. So vague was it, that he dismissed it as imagination. But it persisted and finally he dug spurs into his horse's sides and forced the animal into a lope. Sam wasn't used to unexplained feelings and now this one troubled him.

Sam was six feet tall and weighed a hundred and seventy pounds, all of which was bone, muscle and sinew. There was a thirty-thirty carbine thrust down into a saddle boot beneath his knee and he wore a double-action Colt's forty-five in a holster at his side.

Sam hadn't yet been born at the time of the Civil War. But he'd fought in the Spanish War, and had been with Roosevelt's Rough Riders at the battle of San Juan Hill. He'd been wounded in the thigh, and still bore a white and ugly scar. The wound had become infected because of delay in treating it, and for a time had threatened him with the loss of his leg. He still walked with a slight limp, but otherwise it didn't inconvenience him.

Idly now, he wondered why he hadn't married a long time ago. He'd courted several women in the last ten years, but something had always cooled him off before he actually got around to asking any of them to marry him.

Lily MacDonald was different. She was warm and affectionate. She looked at him as if he was the greatest thing she'd ever seen. She was a good mother and she took the running of her ranch in stride the way she did everything else. It was something that had to be done; she was the one who had to do it and that was that. She was a strong woman but her strength in no way detracted from her womanliness. And in a couple of months, she'd be his wife.

By now, all the light had faded from the sky, leaving only the faint glow that came from the stars.

Sam's feeling of uneasiness increased. What was the matter with him, he asked himself. He was getting to be a damned old woman. Nothing was wrong out at Lily's place. Nothing *could* be wrong.

Nevertheless, he held his horse to a steady lope until the animal began to sweat. Only then did he draw him back to a walk.

With the horse at a walk, he fumed at the delay. He knew, by landmarks he had passed, that he was already more than halfway there. His premonition grew and for several moments he debated the wisdom of going back to town for the doctor. He discarded the idea almost immediately. He'd look like a fool asking Doc Martin to ride all the way out here just because of an unsubstantiated feeling of uneasiness.

He spurred his horse into a lope again, his lean jaw clenched, his eyes narrowed and intense.

*   *   *

There were six wagons in the train. Arch Dillman rode at the head of the column along with Saul Ernst. The heavily laden wagons, their cargoes covered with canvas tarpaulins firmly lashed down, were driven by the others, Jake Gwin, Frank Helder, Phil Hibbert, Chuck Hite, Juan de la Torre, and Rogelio Leon.

In each of the first five wagons were a thousand 30-40 Krags, stolen from a U.S. Army armory six months before. In the sixth were a hundred and fifty thousand rounds of 30-40 ammunition.

All of the men carried rifles and each had a revolver strapped to his side. Dillman had, in addition to the rifle, a double-barreled shotgun and both pockets of his coat sagged with ammunition for it, paper cartridges loaded with 00 buck.

Dillman was a man of medium size, five feet ten inches tall, but stocky and strong from a lifetime of hard ranchwork. Ernst, by contrast, was flabby and soft, and still shifted his weight often to ease the chafed places on the insides of his thighs.

While this was strictly a business deal, Dillman was fully aware that it was not without its risks. The guns were stolen, but they had been in storage for more than a year and their theft had gone undetected. Saul Ernst had bought them for three dollars each, with the ammunition for them thrown in.

Pancho Villa, the Mexican revolutionary, was willing to pay twenty dollars each, and five cents a round for the ammunition. It added up to $107,500 and since the cost had been a mere $15,000, the profit about to be realized was enormous.

And the best part of the deal was that the guns didn't have to be delivered to Mexico, or even to the border between Mexico and the United States. Villa had agreed to take possession of the guns at an isolated ranch three miles north of the border as the crow flies, but more than twenty miles by road.

Dillman had done business with Villa before on a smaller scale. He had also done business with emissaries of Venustiano Carranza. Both times he had been paid either in gold Mexican coins or in U.S. currency. The arrangements were the same this time. Payment was to be made either in gold Mexican coins or in United States currency.

Dillman halted his horse and let the wagons rumble past. Ernst was still shifting uncomfortably around in his saddle, trying to

15

ease the places that had chafed. Dillman didn't like Ernst but he'd had to let the man come along because he hadn't been able to raise the $10,000 Ernst was asking for the guns. Ernst had insisted on coming along to be sure of getting paid. He was to get an extra $5,000 because of the extra risk involved.

Behind Ernst came the first wagon, driven by Jake Gwin. Gwin was a veteran of both the Civil and the Spanish wars. He was grizzled and gray, his face deeply seamed by years. There was a white scar across the top of his head where a bullet had creased it and where no hair would grow. He was wiry and tough. He wasn't an outlaw in the strictest sense and he didn't see anything wrong with supplying guns to the various factions fighting it out in Mexico even though he knew it was illegal. But he did know that the penalty would be prison if he was caught.

Frank Helder drove the second wagon. Helder was big, with eyes that never quite met another man's head-on. Dillman knew Helder was capable of trying to get away with all the money. He wasn't much worried because he didn't figure one man could do it by himself. But he was also aware that Helder might talk one of the others into helping him and he intended to watch Helder closely from the moment the rifles were delivered to Villa and the money paid.

Phil Hibbert drove the third wagon and as he

passed, Hibbert called out cheerfully, 'Everything all right?'

'Yep.'

'Another day and we'll all be rich.'

'Don't count it until you've got it in your hands. A lot can happen.' He was remembering that Hibbert had gotten drunk the night they took delivery of the rifles from Ernst at a deserted barn a dozen miles east of San Angelo. Dillman had found him and hauled him out of the saloon, but he didn't know how much Hibbert had blabbed about the arms deal before he did. He did know that he'd gotten a lot of curious looks from some of the men in the saloon and he wondered if one of them had followed them back to the camp.

Chuck Hite drove the next wagon. Chuck was short and stocky and built like a bull. He had been a teamster all his life. He'd driven caissons during the Civil War, and stagecoaches afterward. Once he'd had a freight line of his own that had gone broke. Now he was hoping to use the money he got from this arms deal to start another line. He had a wife and two kids, but his wife didn't know what he was doing now.

Juan de la Torre drove the next to the last wagon, followed by Rogelio Leon in the last. Neither spoke more than a few words of English and Dillman was most suspicious of these two because he suspected they had ties in Mexico and he didn't know with whom. If they

17

were Carranza's followers, they were dangerous. If they were Villa supporters, he had nothing to worry about.

Dillman didn't know how Villa planned to get the rifles safely across the border and into Mexico but that wasn't his problem.

Dillman was familiar with the locality where the exchange was going to take place. He trusted his men within certain limits and had no real reason to doubt any of them.

Why, then, did he feel so damned uneasy over this particular deal? He made up his mind that he would be more vigilant than usual. Until Villa's gold was safely in his hands.

CHAPTER THREE

Pancho Villa was a big man, six feet tall, weighing over two hundred pounds. Astride a horse, he was a skillful and graceful rider. Afoot, he appeared gangling and awkward. He had warm brown eyes and a wide, sweeping mustache. He could be charming when wooing a woman. He was also capable of ordering mass executions without trials.

So far, his successes had been impressive. His ragtag army of bandits, peons, and volunteers had captured Torreón, Chihuahua City, and Juárez. In Juárez, which he had captured by the simple expedient of having a trainload of coal unloaded and substituting his soldiers for its cargo, he had also captured a considerable amount of gold, American dollars and Mexican pesos when his men raided the city's gambling establishments.

But Villa was aware that he had many enemies among those presently commanding various revolutionary armies. He also knew that northern Mexico was not the place where the war of the revolution would finally be won. It was to the south that he must take his army, to Guadalajara, Mexico City, Puebla, and Vera Cruz.

And to overcome the forces of Huerta and Carranza, he needed many men, whom he hoped to recruit as he went along. Mostly, though, he needed guns, not the old muzzle loaders and percussion guns many of his soldiers carried now, but modern guns, repeaters, the 30-40 Krags that had been used by the United States Army in the Spanish War.

Villa had begun his adult life as a cattle rustler and butcher. He butchered the cattle he stole and sold the meat out of his butcher shop in Juárez. He had no vices, at least none of the minor ones. He cared nothing for tobacco or alcohol. But he had an insatiable appetite for women though he preferred to marry them rather than simply to rape or seduce them. This way, he got all the woman had to give and not simply the temporary satisfaction afforded by her company for a single night. How many times he was married during his adult life is unknown. But later in life he admitted that he had stopped counting at seventy-five.

The name he had been given at birth was Doroteo Arango. When he changed it to Francisco Villa was not clear. But as he rose in the ranks of revolutionary fighters, his ideas of what he could accomplish began to grow. Now he envisioned a march on Mexico City, capturing each sizable town along the way. Then and only then could he say to his beloved 'little President' that the country was secure from Madero's enemies.

After Madero was murdered, Villa's determination did not change. He still hoped to secure the entire country in the name of Madero, for the principles for which Madero had stood. A villain himself, he admired the good for which good men stood. Several times he had bought guns from Dillman, usually fifty or so at a time, and had taken delivery in El Paso, or just across the border in Juárez. He trusted Dillman as much as he trusted any gringo. He supposed that Dillman trusted him about equally, as much as he trusted any greaser.

Villa had about a third of the money he would need to buy the five thousand rifles from Dillman. He had not the slightest idea of where he could get the other two thirds. He knew he couldn't get it in gold, American currency, or pesos backed by the Mexican Government.

But he now had another plan working for him. He had just established a state bank and he had the bank's presses working twenty-four hours a day turning out pesos, the ultimate goal being two million pesos guaranteed by nothing more than Francisco Villa's signature.

He wasn't worried about whether or not the people of Chihuahua would accept the new issue of currency. He had issued a decree, making it the legal tender of the entire state. He had ordered that all gold and pesos currently in circulation be exchanged for it, the penalty for non-compliance being imprisonment or death. But so far all the hard money had not been turned in.

With the new issue of currency he could give his soldiers their back pay. He could buy food, supplies, and whatever guns and ammunition were available to him in Mexico, and he could use the gold and hard currency turned in to buy more guns and ammunition in the United States.

For now he intended to use the new currency to pay Dillman for the five thousand 30-40 Krags he was buying from him. He had ordered that the new peso bills be the same size as American paper currency. He intended to package it with several American bills on each side of each package. He hoped that Dillman and his men, when they accepted the money, would not look too deeply into the packages. If they did—well, he would have sixty or seventy men with him. He could simply have Dillman and his men shot, take the rifles, and the money, and return to Mexico.

On the same night that Ezra Pew took over Lily MacDonald's ranch house, Pancho Villa and his men rode out of Juárez, waiting until after midnight when the soldiers and members of the border patrol, watching the border in the vicinity of El Paso and Juárez would either be sleeping or clustered around their campfires brewing coffee. Villa hoped to avoid a clash with United States troops. Relations between him and the United States were already strained enough.

Silently the cavalcade, with Villa at its head, splashed across the shallow Rio Grande about ten miles south of the two cities. No challenges rang out. The bluffs and hills along the river seemed deserted.

Occasionally a bit would rattle as a horse tossed his head. Or someone's saddle leathers would creak as the rider shifted his weight.

Villa began to think of the logistical difficulties of getting five thousand rifles and a hundred and fifty thousand rounds of ammunition back to Mexico. His seventy-five men couldn't carry them, which meant he would need to commandeer the wagons and teams that had been used by Dillman to transport them to the place where the sale was to take place, an isolated ranch, three miles from the border as the crow flies but twenty miles from it by road.

Now he realized that if he was to move the rifles south to Mexico by wagon, Dillman and his men would have time to divide the money, which meant they would discover it was not, as the agreement provided, American currency.

To Villa, who had lined captured *federales* up for execution four deep so that each bullet would kill four men, the solution was simple and obvious. When they took delivery of the rifles they would simply have to kill Dillman and all his men. Only then could they be sure of enough time to get the slow-moving wagons loaded with rifles and ammunition back to Mexico.

That he meant to double-cross Dillman bothered Villa not at all. He was fighting for Mexico. He was fighting for the principles in which Madero believed, that the land belonged to the poor, not to the rich *haciendados* who lived in extreme luxury while they kept the peons in virtual slavery. Already he had confiscated the land of the Terrazas family and distributed it, in twenty-five hectare plots to those who had formerly worked the land for the Terrazas.

They were due south of El Paso, and so Villa had to lead his men in a big circle around it to avoid detection. Whenever they rode close to an isolated ranch, Villa detoured it, trying to stay on the downwind side so that the ranch horses would not smell his mounts and give the

23

alarm.

The country north of El Paso was extremely rough, with barren, rocky, cactus-covered mountains. Villa's progress was slow. Frequently it was necessary to stop and rest the horses. Villa, who knew that cavalry is only as good as its mounts, saw to it that each time they stopped cinches were loosened and bits taken out of the horses' mouths so that they could crop the scarce, short dry grass that grew on the shady side of the rocks and cactus plants.

*   *   *

Sam Chance slowed his horse to a walk as he approached Lily MacDonald's place. He could see lamplight flickering from the kitchen windows. In the glow it cast on the ground outside, he saw the shapes of several horses. He halted his own horse immediately.

His uneasiness, then, had a cause. At least three men and maybe more were down there in Lily's house.

Frowning, he sat there staring at the house. Who were they and what did they want? Lily MacDonald's ranch was isolated and well off the beaten path.

Frowning, he tried to guess what their purpose might be. Being a lawman, only one conclusion seemed possible. The men were outlaws, wanted men. They had picked Lily's

24

ranch to hide out for a while because it was so remote. They probably didn't know that Sam visited Lily at least once a week.

Sam knew one thing for sure. If they were outlaws, then both Lily and her son were in danger. And so were the two Mexican cowboys who worked for her.

As he watched, the door opened. He could see into the kitchen, which was crowded with men. One man came out, a big, heavy-set man, and closed the door behind him. Sam saw movement among the horses so dimly lighted by the lamplight from the window. Man and horses disappeared. Sam heard the barn door creak.

Which meant they intended to stay all night. Still several hundred yards from the house Sam dismounted and tied his horse to a stout clump of brush. Then he walked slowly down the lane toward the house. Before he reached it, he heard the barn door creak again. He stopped and watched until the man who had put the horses in the barn disappeared inside the house.

He knew he'd be a fool to reveal his presence before he knew what was going on. Cautiously he approached the house. He was still fifty feet away from it when he heard the dog whine. When the dog did not approach, wagging his tail as he usually did, Sam headed in the direction of the whine.

Spot lay on his side, his tail thumping weakly

against the ground. Sam Chance knelt. The dog whined softly as Sam touched his head.

It was obvious that the dog was hurt. It was also obvious to Sam that there was nothing he could do about it now. If he tried to move or help the dog, the animal would yelp and that would draw the strangers from the house.

Sam got to his feet. The dog tried to get up, whimpered with pain, and lay back again. Cautiously Sam circled the house so that if the door should open again he would not be plainly visible.

He knew these were not law-abiding men. He also knew how outlaws usually treated women and he had seen enough to know that this bunch was an unusually dirty and vicious-looking lot.

He knew what he would probably do if one of them molested Lily or put his hands on her. He also knew that such an action would cost him his life and wouldn't help Lily at all.

CHAPTER FOUR

Still uncertain about what he ought to do, Sam Chance moved back into the darkness so that if one of the men inside the house should come to the door, he would not be seen. He was on a direct line with the kitchen window and could see clearly into the room.

So far, none of them seemed to be threatening Lily, and except for the hurt dog, which injury could have resulted from an accident or being kicked by a horse, he had no real reason to believe the men were a threat.

Suddenly he realized that he had not seen Garcia inside the house. Immediately he moved closer so that he could look into every corner of the room.

He saw Ramirez, standing against the wall on the far side of the room. He saw Jimmy, who was staring at one of the men with wide, frightened eyes. And, as he watched, Lily had to pass this same man to get more wood for the stove and he reached out a hand, grinning. She tried to avoid his hand, without complete success.

Sam Chance felt anger rise instantly in his mind. He started to move away from the window and toward the door. Lily shouldn't have to endure that kind of treatment and he meant to see that it stopped.

But as he moved away from the window, he saw something else: the smashed remains of the rifle that had hung over the fireplace on pegs. It had been thrown into the fireplace. Part of the stock had burned but the barrel stuck out, easily identifiable.

The two things came together suddenly. Garcia's absence and the smashed rifle. Garcia must have tried to protect Lily. Usually unarmed, he had reached for the rifle above the

27

mantel. Now the rifle was smashed and Garcia missing. Unless he was lying wounded in the bedroom, he must be dead.

Sam knew then that his first instinct had been right. These were dangerous men and if he barged in, alone, to try protecting Lily from them, he'd be shot down with no hesitation at all.

Moving back once more, he continued to watch as Lily prepared supper for them. He had counted six. Regardless of what happened in there, he would have to bide his time and wait until he had some chance of succeeding and would not simply be throwing his life away.

Later, maybe he'd have a chance at them, one or two at a time. And yet even as he had that thought, he knew it was useless. They had Lily and Jimmy and men like these wouldn't hesitate to use them as hostages, threatening either torture or death if Sam didn't surrender himself.

Carefully avoiding the man who had tried to paw her, Lily now carried the meal to the table and the men got up and sat down at it. None of them came outside to wash.

Sam waited a few moments more, until all had been served and had begun to eat. Then, hurrying, he left the window and headed for the barn. The dog, Spot, whined faintly as he passed.

Inside the barn there was a lantern, hanging

on a nail beside the door. He struck a match and lighted it. Holding it high above his head, he made a circle of the barn. Except for the six loose horses nothing seemed different. But there was a pile of hay in the back corner that had been thrown down from the loft. He reached it and stirred it with his foot.

His boot encountered something solid. Kneeling, he put the lantern down on the barn floor and began pawing the hay aside. He uncovered the body of a man, legs first, torso next, and finally the face. It was Garcia. He was dead. He had been shot in the chest. There was a spot of blood as big as Sam's hand on his chest that was already beginning to dry and turn dark.

Fury smoldered now in Sam. He had liked Heraldo Garcia and had known him ever since Garcia had come to work out here several years ago. One of the outlaws must have been pawing Lily and Garcia had done, however foolishly, what any decent man would do. He had tried for the gun over the fireplace and before he could put his hands on it, he had been shot.

Sam clenched his teeth as he swiftly covered Garcia over again with hay. He got up, picked up the lantern and blew it out. He returned it to its nail beside the door.

He knew that the next hours were going to be the hardest in his life. He was probably going to have to watch while Lily was mistreated, and

29

he would have to restrain himself because he was Lily's only hope and he'd be no good to her if he was dead.

He compromised those thoughts even as he had them. If the molesting was restricted to pawing and pinching and ribald jokes, then he could probably control himself. But if any of them began ripping the clothes from her, then that man was going to be dead. But even as he made that promise to himself, he asked himself the question, 'And afterward? What then? Who's going to help her then?'

He stepped out of the barn into the darkness. Fuming inwardly, he made his way back to the house, circling it so that he would not be surprised by one of the outlaws coming out of the kitchen door.

Moving around on the other side, he again took up his place about twenty feet from the window so that he would not be illuminated by its light. Lily was cleaning up the table now, carrying the dishes from the table to the work counter beside the stove where the dishpan was.

Every time she passed the man who had pawed her before, he grinned and tried to do it again. Finally, exasperated, Lily raised the stack of dishes she was carrying above her head and brought the whole stack down squarely on the seated man's head.

Stunned, he fell off the chair. The other five men began to laugh. The man Lily had struck with the dishes got up off the floor, his expression murderous. He started across the room toward her. She picked up the dishpan of water heating on the stove, readying it to throw into his face. Sam moved closer to the window so as to be able to get off a clear shot if necessary.

The huge, gray-bearded man at the kitchen table said harshly, 'Hines!'

Hines turned his head. He said, 'I'll show that bitch. I'll...'

'You'll do nothing. We need her here. And that other Mexican, too. What are Dillman and his friends going to think if nobody's here when they arrive?'

'Did you see what she did to me?'

Pew grinned, but there was no humor in the grin. He said, 'Take a look at what she's going to do to you.'

'Damn it, you can't tell me...'

There suddenly was a gun in Pew's huge hand. 'I can kill you. Then we'll only have to split that money five ways instead of six.'

Hines hesitated, staring at Pew, his own hand tensed and close to his gun. Then his body relaxed as he realized he would be dead before his hand could touch his gun. He shrugged. 'All right, all right. No need to get so goddam touchy about it.'

Pew grinned, 'Besides, that water's hot enough to take the hide off you.'

The other men laughed. All but one. He was

watching Lily in a strange and speculative way. Pew ordered Hines to move out of the way and Lily gathered up the dishes she had struck Hines with, some broken, some not. Those that were unbroken she stacked with the others on the worktable. The broken ones she threw into the trash box beside the stove.

She poured hot water into another dishpan, then put a bar of soap into the dishwater. She put some of the dishes in and began to wash. Jimmy came, without having to be called, and picked up the flour-sack dish-towel. As his mother washed and rinsed the dishes, he took them from her and dried them. There were a lot of dishes because a lot of people had eaten supper. It occurred to Sam that neither Lily nor Jimmy had eaten anything. They were both too scared he thought, and probably had no appetite.

Sam had never felt so helpless in his life. He needed help to handle this situation but there was no time to go for help. By the time he rode to town, raised a posse and came back, whatever was happening here would probably be over with. Lily would be dead, having been raped repeatedly before she was killed. Ramirez and Jimmy would also be dead.

Sam backed away from the window again now that the crisis between Lily and Hines was over with. He tried, standing in the darkness, to figure out what was going on. He'd heard enough to know that a group of men, led by someone named Dillman, was due to arrive here at Lily's ranch, and that Pew wanted things to look normal when they did. To this end, he would probably leave Lily and Ramirez in the house and take Jimmy with him as a hostage to make sure they didn't give him and his men away.

So far, so good. But who was Dillman, and why was he coming here? That was something he would have to find out. And when was he due to arrive? Nothing specific had been said, but he'd gotten the impression that Dillman and his men were due tonight, and that a lot of money was involved.

He could hear Spot, who could both see and smell him in spite of the darkness, whining. He crossed the yard to the dog and knelt. With gentle hands, he went over the dog's head, neck, back, and legs, probing to see where the injury was. Only when he touched the dog's side did Spot let out a small yelp of pain. Sam petted his head absently and got to his feet. He thought about carrying the dog to the barn, then put the thought out of his mind. If the dog was moved, the outlaws would suspect that someone was around. Particularly if they studied the ground for tracks.

He returned carefully to the window. His curiosity was now thoroughly aroused but it wasn't curiosity that made him realize he had to know more about what was going on. There wasn't much affirmative action he could take, unless he knew what was going to happen here.

He was in time to hear a little, dried-up man with eyes as cold as those of a snake, ask, 'What time you figure they'll be getting here?'

Pew glanced at him. There was a different expression in Pew's face when he looked at this man than when he looked at Hines. It was almost a look of respect. He said, 'I don't know, Les. Those five wagons have each got a thousand rifles in them and that's a lot of weight. The last wagon has got over a hundred and fifty thousand rounds of ammunition. They've each got four mules on them but the mules have got to be getting tired. I'd say a couple of hours before dawn.'

Sam's mind did a little swift arithmetic. A thousand guns in each of five wagons added up to five thousand guns. And there was no place where five thousand guns could be sold except south of the border in Mexico.

That meant Francisco Villa. His was the only revolutionary army within several hundred miles that could use that many guns.

It all began to drop into place and make some sense. Villa had made a deal with Dillman to supply him with five thousand guns, probably stolen from a U.S. Army arsenal someplace. Delivery was to be made here because this ranch was isolated and also because it was only three miles from the border cross country even if it was fifteen or twenty by road.

But somewhere along the line, something, some news of the plan had leaked out. Chance was reasonably sure that this bunch of unsavory killers was not a part of the original plan. Someone, one of Dillman's men, must have let something slip, probably while he was drunk. Pew and his five murderous companions had located the wagons, maybe by following the drunk with the blabbermouth. They had followed long enough to ascertain where the wagons were headed and then had hurried on ahead in order to lay an ambush for them.

Or perhaps an ambush was not exactly what they had in mind. Pew had said he wanted things to look natural. That might mean he intended to let the gun sale take place. Then, after Villa and his men had paid the money over to Dillman and departed with the guns, Pew could move in, take the money and murder Dillman, all his men, Lily MacDonald and Ramirez. When the bodies were discovered it would simply be assumed that the Villistas were the murderers and the infamy already attached to the name of Pancho Villa would go up a notch or two.

Sam felt sure that he had, at last, figured out what was going on. Again he did a little mental arithmetic. He had no way of knowing what kind of guns Dillman was bringing Villa, but the ones available in U.S. Army arsenals right now would probably be 30-40 Krags left over from the Spanish War. They were good guns, good enough for an army, and Villa would be anxious to get as many of them as he could. He'd probably be willing to pay fifteen or twenty dollars apiece, if the guns were new.

That added up to around a hundred thousand dollars, plus whatever Villa paid for the hundred and fifty thousand rounds of ammunition. Enough to make this gang of killers absolutely merciless.

Inside the kitchen, Lily finished with the dishes, took the dishtowel from Jimmy, and hung it up on a rack beside the stove to dry.

Jimmy was looking up at her and there were tears running down his cheeks. She knelt to comfort him. Sam Chance couldn't understand Jimmy's words because he was crying so.

CHAPTER FIVE

Twice, while Jimmy was pleading with her, Lily looked across the room at Pew. Finally a certain firmness came to her mouth. She said, 'My son wants to take his dog into the barn and make him a bed of hay.'

Pew shook his head. Lily's face flushed with anger. She said, 'Either you let me take him out and carry the dog to the barn or you can get your own damn meals from now on.'

Sam felt a small grin touch his mouth. Lily was a woman of spirit, that was sure. If slamming the dishes down on Hines's head hadn't already proved it, this did.

Pew said, 'Don't get uppity with me, woman, or I'll let Hines have you.'

'No you won't. Because you need me to make whoever's coming here think that nothing is wrong.'

Pew's glance at her took on a certain reluctant respect. He said, 'All right. Go ahead and take the dog into the barn. Somebody go with her.'

Hines said, 'I'll go.'

Pew said, 'Better keep your distance from her, Hines.'

Hines's face flushed irritably. Lily took Jimmy by the hand and went to the door. Hines followed. Pew said, 'Hines.'

The man turned his head. Pew said, 'If she comes back in here with a mark on her where it shows, I'll either kill you or beat hell out of you. Keep it in mind.'

Hines only scowled. He went out the door, following Lily, grabbing a lantern from a nail beside the door as he did. Just outside, he stopped long enough to light the lantern. Lily and Jimmy went at once to where the dog was still lying.

Sam was tempted. This was a chance to get rid of Hines and improve Lily's chances of coming through this unmolested. Yet even as

37

he had the thought, he knew it wouldn't work. The shot would bring the five running from the house. They'd come out shooting and the chance of Lily or Jimmy being hit was too great a risk.

The dog whimpered pitifully as Lily gathered him into her arms and headed for the adobe-walled barn. Hines came along behind with the lantern and opened the door for her. Sam stayed far enough back so that he was untouched by the lantern light. The three went in and Hines pulled the door closed behind him so that the horses would not get out.

Sam approached the barn door. The dog was whining with the pain and Jimmy was crying now with sympathy. Sam peered through the crack between the door and the jamb.

Lily crossed the barn. There was a buggy parked against one wall, its shafts resting on the floor. She laid the dog down gently underneath the buggy, then crossed the barn after an armload of hay.

Returning, she put the hay down, spread it out to make a small bed for the dog. She gently lifted the animal onto it. Jimmy stopped crying long enough to ask, 'Hadn't we ought to get him some food? Or some water or something?'

'I don't think so, Jimmy. He's hurting too much to eat or drink right now. But maybe tomorrow ...' Her voice trailed off, probably because she realized that by tomorrow none of them had much chance of still being alive.

Hines stood with his back to the door, the lantern in his hand, blocking it. He said, 'Go on back to the house, kid. Your ma and me will be along pretty soon.'

Jimmy looked up at his mother, knuckling the tears out of his eyes. Lily hesitated.

Hines said, 'It don't make a damn bit of difference to me whether he's here or not. Maybe it don't make no difference to you, either.'

Lily, her face pale and her voice trembling, said, 'Jimmy, go on back to the house. It's all right. I'll be along in a few minutes.'

Hines laughed. 'Might take longer than that.'

Jimmy hesitated and Lily repeated more firmly, 'Go on back to the house, Jimmy. Do what I say. Now!'

Reluctantly Jimmy headed for the barn door. Hines let him through and Sam moved out of the way enough so that when the boy came out he would not be seen. Hines, who was already heading toward Lily, called after the boy, 'Shut the door.'

Jimmy went toward the house but he did not shut the door. Hines, with a muttered curse, came to close the door and dropped the bar into place. There was a wide enough crack between the door and the jamb so that Sam could see most of the inside.

He knew Hines was going to rape Lily and he

39

wasn't going to stand by while it happened, no matter what the later consequences might be. Sam slid his revolver from the holster and shoved the muzzle through the crack in the door. He could use it this way, but the best solution would be to swing the door wide, shoot Hines, and then drive the horses out.

Slowly, silently, he pulled on the latchstring, raised the bar and opened the barn door slightly. He knew the door would squeak when he opened it, and that would turn Hines toward him. The man would probably go for his gun but it wasn't going to do him any good.

One thing Sam knew he had to do. He had to kill Hines before he actually got hold of Lily. Otherwise Hines would use her as a shield and shoot from behind her at him.

Sam's hands were shaking with fury and his body felt as if all the blood had drained out of it. Hines hung the lantern from a nail and approached Lily, who retreated in a circle so he couldn't corner her.

He made a sudden rush, and she turned and ran, holding up her skirt with one hand so that it wouldn't trip her. Hines laughed and stopped running, and Lily stopped too, turning again to face him.

Her face was as terrified as that of a cornered bird. Her voice was thin with terror as she said, 'He'll kill you. He said he would.'

'I ain't going to mark up your face.' He was getting closer all the time, probably because

Lily was backing up and he was moving forward toward her. She kept trying to circle and stay out of corners, but he kept edging her back toward the rear of the barn where the pile of hay and Heraldo Garcia's body were. He meant to back her into that hay, Sam thought furiously, and take her right next to where Heraldo's body lay.

Sam opened the door far enough to admit his body and stepped into the barn. The hammer of his gun made a click, but Hines was now too intent to hear anything. He had Lily backed into the corner from which there was no escape. He was only a dozen feet away from her and could catch her in a single rush.

Sam raised his gun, sighting it as well as he could in the faint light coming from the lantern.

In that instant, Lily's foot touched something she immediately recognized as the handle of the pitchfork. Stooping, before Hines realized what she was doing, she straightened, holding it with both hands, the three rusty tines pointing at Hines. Her voice was shrill with terror, but it had a strong, determined ring. 'All right, Mr Hines. If you think it's worth three holes in your belly, come on.'

For a moment, Hines stopped. He stood there a moment, motionless, hesitating between his lust for Lily and his fear of the sharp tines of the fork. Finally, apparently deciding he could wrench the thing from her before she could hurt him with it, he began to advance again.

Sam quickly moved aside, and resting his gun arm on the partition that made up one of the few stalls in the barn, he took a bead on Hines's chest. His finger tightened on the trigger and he opened his mouth to call out to Hines, knowing the instant he did, Hines would go for his gun.

He was momentarily distracted by the sudden surge of the horses away from the door where they had bunched. He turned his head.

Someone had come in. Hines saw him at the same time Sam did and halted his advance toward Lily. Sam wished she would lunge, right now, with the pitchfork, and end Hines's threat to her once and for all but he knew that she would not. Strong she might be, but she was neither violent nor could she hurt anything or anyone except in her own defense or in the defense of someone she loved.

It was Quigley who had come in the door. He saw what was going on and said in a cold, level voice, 'Get the hell away from her before I blow you apart!'

Hines didn't move, but he growled, 'What the devil are you doing here?'

'When the kid came in, Pew sent me out. Damn it, he told you he'd kill you if you put any marks on her.'

'I wasn't going to put any marks on her. At

least not where they'd show.'

Sam stood frozen in the shadows beside the stall partition. He didn't dare to move for fear Quigley's eye would catch the movement. He knew he probably was almost invisible in the near darkness inside the barn. The only reason Hines and Lily were visible to Quigley was that the lantern hung within a dozen feet of them.

Quigley's voice took on a menace it had not possessed before while still remaining very steady and soft. He said, 'Get away from her or pull your gun. You got half a minute to make up your mind.'

Hines took only half the allotted time. Then he said, 'Oh hell, what's all the fuss? She's only a goddam woman!'

Quigley didn't reply. Hines turned away from Lily and headed straight toward Quigley. Quigley stepped aside, for the moment turning his back to Sam. Sam took the opportunity to duck down behind the stall partition.

Abreast of Quigley, Hines muttered, 'You sonofabitch, I'll get you for this.'

'Anytime.'

Hines went on toward the door. Quigley said, 'Come on, Mrs MacDonald. Come on back into the house.'

She released the pitchfork. Unsteadily, she walked toward Quigley. He passed her and got the lantern from the nail where Hines had hung it. Hines banged out the door, slamming it savagely behind him. Quigley, coming toward it with the lantern in his hand, grinned. 'Mad, isn't he?'

Lily did not reply. Sam looked at her terror-stricken face and wished he could reveal his presence to reassure her. But he didn't dare. His only chance lay in the fact that none of the outlaws knew that he was here. The horses crowded past Quigley and bunched in the far rear corner of the barn.

Going out the door, Sam heard Quigley say puzzledly, 'Sure seems like I've seen you someplace before.'

And he heard Lily's voice, 'Someone that looked like me, maybe. I've lived right here for over five years.'

'Where'd you come from before that?'

Sam didn't hear her reply because Quigley dropped the bar into place just as she spoke. Sam waited a few moments and then stepped out of the barn.

Nearly to the house, Quigley said, 'You sure you've never been in San Antonio?'

'I'm sure.' Her voice was trembling. Quigley was certain he had seen her in San Antonio. He had been there for a couple of years, and he'd been pretty interested in a certain saloon girl there, a very young one who had looked just like Lily might have looked six years before.

She seemed disturbed now when he pressed her about it but that might be because she was still badly shaken by the near escape she'd had from Hines. He smiled slightly to himself. He

44

had to admire the way she'd been holding Hines off with that pitchfork. He wondered if she'd really have rammed it into him. He was willing to bet she would or at least would have tried her best.

Ahead of them, the door of the house opened and Hines went in, leaving the door ajar. Quigley watched Lily as she went into the lighted door. He remembered the girl in San Antonio and suddenly he wanted this woman more than he had wanted any woman since. He wanted her and he'd have her before they left this place, but he didn't intend to be as crude about it as Hines. Maybe if he let her think he was defending her she'd come to him willingly. If not, well hell, there was always the other way.

He didn't like Hines anyhow and killing him would be a pleasure. Furthermore, he had a hunch none of the others, Pew included, would mind if Hines was out of the way. It would just mean a bigger share of the money for those that were left.

And anyway, it was a matter of survival with Quigley. If he didn't kill Hines, sooner or later Hines was going to kill him.

He closed the door behind him. Jimmy was standing in the far corner of the room, his face streaked with tears. Lily said, 'It's time he was in bed. Does anybody object...?'

Pew said, 'Go ahead and put him to bed. We'll have to get him up though, after a while,

45

so leave him dressed.'

She went to Jimmy and took him into the bedroom that opened off the kitchen. She was gone about ten minutes. When she finally emerged, she seemed steadier than she had before.

Pew said, 'You didn't put that kid out the window, did you?' He heaved his huge frame up from the chair where he was sitting and, picking up the lamp, went into the bedroom. He returned to the kitchen, satisfied that Jimmy was still in the house.

Lily wished she'd thought of lowering Jimmy from the window. On second thought, she decided it wouldn't have done any good. He couldn't run fast enough or hide well enough to escape a search by these six men. Hopelessly, she considered what lay ahead, for her, for Jimmy, and for Ramirez, who still sat gloomily in a straight-backed chair.

CHAPTER SIX

Outside, by the barn, Sam Chance watched as Hines, Lily, and Quigley disappeared into the house. Immediately he crossed the yard and again took up his position a dozen or so feet from the kitchen window, from where he could see most of the kitchen's interior. He saw Lily lead Jimmy, whose face was still streaked with tears, into the bedroom. He saw Ramirez, sitting in a straight-backed chair, his face disconsolate. Ramirez was, he knew, no more lacking in courage than Garcia had been, and if Garcia hadn't gone for the rifle, Ramirez would have. But neither was he stupid and he realized that getting himself killed now would do nobody any good. Sam hoped he would continue to be able to control himself because alive he could be crucially valuable later on.

Sam eased closer to the window. He felt irritated at himself, skulking in the darkness, watching what was going on but unable to intervene or change what was happening. But he also knew he had no other choice.

Pew spoke, ordering two of the men to go outside and take up positions as guards. One of those so assigned he called Joe, a stocky, muscular man of about thirty. He told Joe to walk up the lane to the main road and, the instant he heard the approach of the slow-moving wagons, to return at a run so that they could all get out of the house before the wagons and their escort came into sight. He ordered a second man, whom he called Les, to climb the hill behind the house, settle himself in a good spot, and make sure no scouts sneaked up on the isolated adobe house from the rear or from either side.

The two men came out. Sam, having moved back so that he would not be seen, saw them disappear into the darkness. He remained

47

motionless for several minutes afterward, until the sound of their boots scuffing the dirt had faded away.

Standing as close as he dared, and out of the shaft of light that came from the window, Sam now waited, listening to the talk inside the house. Lily sat silently near Ramirez. The outlaws talked, some of them about what they were going to do with all the money they intended to get out of this deal, others about how the thing had come about, still others expressing doubts as to how it might turn out.

From their snatches of talk, Sam was able finally to piece the whole thing together.

Les Chisum had been curious the night Hibbert had bragged about the money he would soon have and had followed the drunk and Dillman back to their camp.

What he found was a camp well hidden in the bed of a dry stream, surrounded by willows and heavy brush. Through the brush, illuminated by the single fire the men had, he was able to make out six wagons and a sizable number of mules.

Now Les was really interested. Hidden out this way, it was likely that the wagons contained some kind of contraband. And the drunk in the saloon had talked about getting rich.

Cautiously Les worked himself closer and closer to the camp, leaving his horse tied a quarter mile away, until finally, hidden in thick brush, he was able to make out most of what was being said around the fire.

The wagons contained five thousand 30-40 Krag rifles, stolen from a U.S. Army arsenal six months before. A man named Dillman, the leader of the group, had ridden to Mexico to negotiate for their sale to Pancho Villa, the revolutionary commander. An agreement had been reached. Villa would pay twenty dollars each for the rifles, five cents a round for the ammunition, delivered at an isolated ranch only three miles from the border by horseback, twenty by road. Delivery was to take place two weeks hence.

Les returned to his friends and told Pew what he had heard. Not knowing the location of the ranch where the exchange was to take place, the band had followed the wagons' trail, certainly no difficult task. Two days before the date set for the exchange, they had forged ahead. There was only one narrow, two-track road and there could not be many ranches in this nearly deserted country that would fit the description of the place where the exchange was to be made.

The road led them to the lane that branched off to Lily MacDonald's ranch. Now they were waiting for the wagons to arrive. But they didn't intend to attack the men with the rifles until after the exchange with Villa had taken place because there was a chance Villa would bring a small army and simply take the rifles by

49

force, killing the men who had brought them there. Because of that possibility, they meant to wait until Villa had paid the money and gone. That way they could minimize the risk to themselves.

What was to follow was calculated, cold-blooded murder. They planned to kill every one of the men who had brought the rifles here. And while they didn't say it outright because of Lily's presence and that of Ramirez, they would also kill Lily, Ramirez, and Lily's son. When the bodies were discovered, it would be assumed that Villa and his men had committed the atrocity. Certainly it would not be the first violent act attributed to the Mexican revolutionist. This outlaw gang, under Pew's leadership, would have the money and would not even be wanted for the crime. It was a virtually perfect plan, depending for its success only on the utter ruthlessness of Pew and those who followed him.

The options available to Sam Chance were few and all of them unworkable because of the time element. There was no time to return to town, raise a posse and return. Nor was there time to ride to the nearest army post in El Paso and alert the commandant. If he did that, Villa might be caught and the rifles confiscated. But Lily, Ramirez, and Jimmy would be dead. The truth was, Sam didn't give a damn whether Villa got the rifles or not. He was interested only in saving the lives of Lily, Jimmy, and

50

Ramirez.

*   *   *

Lily MacDonald sat half a dozen feet away from Pedro Ramirez. Both of them were glumly silent, both afraid. Pedro had seen Garcia shot down before his eyes. It had certainly, she thought, done something to his own courage and self-esteem. Pedro Ramirez was no coward but neither was he a fool.

She was still deathly afraid of Hines and of what he wanted to do to her, and she knew that if the wagons containing the rifles did not come within a reasonable time, she was in danger not only from Hines but from the others as well. They had all been a long time on the trail.

But there was a greater danger when the wagons did arrive. Pew and his companions would take Jimmy and leave the house. They would leave her and Pedro Ramirez behind to make things look normal and natural. But she would know, and so would Pedro, that if she gave them away, they would kill Jimmy instantly.

But if she did not give them away, not only the gunrunners but she, Jimmy, and Pedro would be murdered as soon as Villa, his soldiers, and the wagons were gone.

There seemed to be no solution. They were all going to die no matter what she did or did not do.

51

Glancing up, she caught Quigley staring at her. She met his glance briefly, determinedly, then looked away again.

He had recognized her, even after six years had passed. She didn't remember him but he remembered her. From the days when she had worked in the Longhorn Saloon in San Antonio.

It was painful remembering those times. But they were six years past, and a person ought to be able to forget the past sometime, or at least eventually live it down.

She'd quit the Longhorn Saloon a couple of months before meeting Mike MacDonald. At first he hadn't known that she had ever worked in a saloon. But when he asked her to marry him, she had told him the truth.

She couldn't honestly say it had made no difference to him. It had. He'd left her that day, in silence, and she'd thought she had seen the last of him. But next day he had been back, knocking at her door. 'You're a fine woman, Lily. I've known that ever since I met up with you. What you done and where you worked before we met is no concern of mine. I've done a few things myself I ain't shoutin' all over town. I just hope you'll forgive the way I ran off and left you yesterday. And I'm still asking you to marry me.'

Well, she had married him because she was in love with him. She'd been happy with him and she'd made him happy with her. She knew she had. But now the past had returned to haunt her all over again. Would Sam Chance react with as much generosity as Mike MacDonald had? She hoped he would and thought he would but she wasn't sure.

She supposed she'd never know. Sam Chance was in town. She and Jimmy were here and by the time Sam Chance rode out here again to visit her, she and Jimmy would both be dead.

Why hadn't she lowered Jimmy from the window a while ago, she asked herself. She simply hadn't thought of it. Or if she had, and by now she couldn't even be sure whether she had or not, she hadn't done it because she'd felt Jimmy had no chance of escaping six determined men who would be out looking for him. But now she knew she should have tried. Because getting Jimmy away was the only chance she had.

She got up. Pew asked, 'Where you think you're goin'?'

'Jimmy must be having a bad dream. I heard him call out.'

'I didn't hear anything.'

'Well I did.' She headed for the bedroom door. She didn't dare look back to see if any of them were following. She went into the dark bedroom and closed the door behind her.

Jimmy was in bed but he was not asleep. She knelt beside him and whispered, 'Jimmy, I'm going to lower you out of the window. I want

53

you to run to your cave down on the riverbank. You go inside and don't you make a sound no matter what you hear. Will you promise me?'

His voice was small and scared. 'Uh huh.'

'All right. Come on.' She snatched a blanket off the bed. 'I'll throw this out the window after you. Take it along so you won't get cold.'

'Ma, I'm scared.'

'I'm scared too. Come on, out the window you go.'

She opened the window and prepared to lift him out.

The room was suddenly flooded with light. Pew's huge bulk filled the doorway. He said, 'Hey, none of that!'

He crossed the room, grabbed Jimmy from her, and said harshly, 'You get back in bed, kid.' His grip on Lily's arm almost made her cry out with pain. 'Get on back in the other room. Next time you try that I'm going to let you have it right in the teeth.'

Jimmy was back in bed. She picked up the blanket and, pulling her arm angrily away from Pew, spread it over her son. Pew said, 'Leave the door open. I don't give a damn whether the kid gets any sleep or not. Just so he don't get away.'

She patted Jimmy's head reassuringly before she followed Pew out into the kitchen again. Pedro had raised his head, but there didn't seem to be any fight in him. Hines was grinning, letting his eyes rove over her in a way that made her feel undressed. Quigley seemed to have lost interest in her, at least for now.

Jimmy probably couldn't have made it to the river anyway, she thought. The man called Les, up on the hillside, would have spotted him.

But she'd had to try. She wouldn't have been able to live with herself if she hadn't tried.

CHAPTER SEVEN

Standing out in the darkness, Sam couldn't stop the uneasy wandering of his thoughts. What in God's name could he do? What would be effective and successful? What good would one man be against six, particularly when they held a hostage or hostages that were dear to him?

Should he get rid of the two guards Pew had sent out? He could probably find Joe and kill him, and after that find Les and kill him too. But he wouldn't be likely to kill both of them without shots being fired, and shots would bring the others out. They'd find his tracks; they'd know he had been watching them and they'd force Lily to tell them who he was. Maybe he could shoot one or even two more when they came out after him. But when those remaining threatened death or torture to Lily and her son, he'd not be able to stand out here and watch them carry out their threats. He'd have to surrender himself and in their fury over the spoilage of their plan, they'd probably kill him, Lily, and Jimmy, and Pedro immediately.

No. That course was too risky and offered too slim a chance of success. He'd have to wait, and hope, and maybe later something would turn up. The guns would probably arrive sometime after dawn. Villa and his men would certainly not arrive in the dark, since Villa was too smart to ride into an unknown situation without being able to see anything. So it would be early morning before the exchange was complete and Villa left with the guns. Briefly he considered trying to contact Villa before the Mexican revolutionary made contact with the gun smugglers. He gave that idea up immediately. Chances were he'd be shot before he had a chance to talk with Villa at all. Besides that, his Spanish was not fluent enough to be sure of being immediately understood. And to be immediately understood would be absolutely essential if he was to survive.

Silently and bitterly he cursed. There seemed to be nothing he could do. Nothing that had any chance of success.

Hines was still watching Lily, in much the same way a cat might watch a bird. She looked decidedly uncomfortable and stared steadily at the floor to avoid having to look at Hines. The man moved his chair over close to her and began talking very softly to her, so softly that Sam doubted if anyone but Lily could even hear.

But the things he said turned her face a painful red and they made Sam's fury grow nearly out of control. He had to do something. He *had.* to! Anything that would change the way things were going now.

And suddenly he knew what it was. He turned, moving well back from the window as he did, and headed for the barn. He was careful to move slowly, so that no sudden movement would be picked up by the sentry on the hill. He reached the barn, slowly and cautiously raised the bar by pulling on the length of rope hanging outside, and slipped inside.

The horses had apparently become used to the smell of blood from Garcia's body beneath the pile of hay in the rear corner of the place. They were bunched back there, but eating the hay farthest from where his body lay. When Sam approached, they edged away, one kicking out at another that crowded him too close.

Sam thought about moving Garcia's body. He decided against it because he didn't want to leave the outlaws with proof that the fire he intended to start had been anything but an accident. For the same reason, he didn't dare move Jimmy's dog. He'd just have to hope that Lily and Jimmy would be able to rescue the dog before the fire got too hot. He'd have to hope that Ramirez would drag Garcia's body out, before it got burned.

This had to look as if Hines or Quigley had knocked out the ashes of a pipe while they were in the barn. Or that somehow the lantern, put down momentarily on the floor, had started some manure smoldering. Furthermore, it had to be lit in such a way that he could get out of the barn and clear before the fire was seen by the sentry on the hill.

The horses had scattered the hay and trampled some of it. Sam carefully built a small inverted cone out of dry manure. Then, lighting a match, he touched it to some of the dry manure, blowing on it as he did. The stuff did not burst into flame but burned with a glow, like a wood fire that had burned itself down to a bed of coals.

He blew out the match, but did not drop it on the floor. He stuck it into his mouth, holding it between his teeth while he mounded hay over the smoldering manure.

Sam Chance had had experience with fires smoldering in dry manure. He knew they almost never went out. He knew that the glowing fire would spread, and dig deeper into the dry manure underneath, until finally, when it reached something flammable, like straw or hay, it would burst into flame. Sam also knew that the horses would not again come near the hay because of the smell of smoke.

Swiftly now, Sam returned to the door of the barn, opened it and slipped out, carefully lowering the bar into place from outside. He didn't return to the house but instead moved out away from both house and barn until he came to the creek. He slid down the cutbank until he was completely hidden from sight.

And now he waited, staring at the barn. No light showed in the window on this side of it. Up on the hill, he saw the brief glow of a match as the sentry lighted a pipe.

Ten minutes passed, and still no light showed behind the window of the barn. Sam became concerned. He began to worry that the fire he had started so carefully in the dry manure might not flare up and ignite the hay over it.

Then, nearly fifteen minutes after he had left the barn, he heard the horses making an increased racket inside the barn. Their neighs were shrill and filled with terror. The sounds of their galloping back and forth, slamming into the walls and kicking against them, must have been audible even inside the house.

Almost immediately afterward, Sam saw a glow in the window of the barn. He had succeeded after all. Now he would just have to hope that the fire would not be discovered until it was beyond the men's ability to extinguish it.

Apparently the noise of the frightened horses was not as loud as he had supposed, or else there was talk going on in the house that kept them from hearing it. The man Pew had sent up the road would be out of earshot, but the sentry up on the hill should be able to hear about as well as Sam.

But there was no reason why a little scuffling among the horses should upset this man. The pile of hay was small and there were six horses competing for a share of it. A certain amount of scuffling and fighting was normal.

Nor was there a window on the side of the barn that faced the hill. Therefore, that sentry shouldn't be aware of the blaze until it actually broke through the walls or until some light showed through any cracks there might be in the walls of the barn.

Sam wished he could have gotten the dog out before setting the blaze. It occurred to him now, too late, that he could at least have carried Spot to the front of the barn near the doors. It would have been assumed he had made it that far on his own, despite his hurts.

Light was very bright in the window facing Sam and he could smell smoke plainly before a cry went up suddenly from the sentry on the hill. The horses inside the barn were almost crazy by now, thundering back and forth, neighing with terror, rearing and kicking against the confining walls.

Yelling, the sentry, who Sam had heard called Les, ran down the hill toward the house. He was heard before he reached it and the kitchen door opened. Carrying his rifle, Pew came out, followed by two of the other three outlaws inside the house.

'What the hell's all the yelling about?'

60

'The barn! It's on fire!'

Pew uttered a stream of angry profanity. He ran toward the barn, followed by the others, by Lily and Ramirez and, belatedly, by Jimmy. Pew opened the door of the barn and the horses, crazy with fear, came thundering out, knocking him and one of the others down in their rush. Sam thought fleetingly, 'By God, they're afoot,' but Quigley caught the last of the horses by his halter as he thundered past and he hung on, being dragged nearly fifty feet before he could bring the horse to a stop. Pew turned his head and bawled, 'Drive them other horses into the corral. Then come and help us fight this goddam thing.'

Lily ran past him into the barn. Jimmy tried to follow, but Ramirez caught his arm and held him back. Lily was out almost immediately, the dog, Spot, cradled in her arms. Sam heaved a sigh of relief. He would have hated being responsible for the death of Jimmy's dog.

As soon as Lily came out, Ramirez released Jimmy and ran into the blazing interior of the barn himself. Pew was bawling, 'Get some buckets and fill them with water. Get moving, goddam it! We don't want those gunrunners showing up to find the barn on fire!'

The men dispersed to get buckets and fill them at the pump. Lily, carrying the dog, with Jimmy clinging to her skirt, began to edge away from the door of the barn toward the darkness. She almost made it. She was thirty or

61

forty feet from the barn before Hines yelled, 'Oh no you don't. Come back here, you damned sly bitch!'

Sam touched his gun. He would have liked nothing better than to shoot Hines but he let his hand fall away. Lily had withstood more than a few epithets. Hines ran after her, grabbed her arm, and dragged her back toward the fire. Jimmy began to cry with fear.

Back at the fire, Pew roared at Hines, 'Go on! Find yourself a bucket and fill it with water. I'll watch the woman.'

Ramirez came out of the barn, dragging the body of Garcia. Both his clothing and Garcia's were smoldering. Ramirez ran to the pump, seized a bucket of water from a man who was filling it, and dumped it over his head. Then he went back to where Garcia lay and, taking off his wet shirt, put out the smoldering places on Garcia's clothing with it.

The first of the men arrived with a bucket of water. Pew yelled, 'Get to the back of the barn and douse that hay before the fire reaches the hay in the loft!'

But his orders were useless. The blaze had already reached the hay in the loft. The man came out almost immediately, his bucket empty, and yelled over the roar of the flames, 'It's too late. The fire's already in the loft.'

Sam didn't know how much good he'd done by burning Lily's barn. Maybe none at all. But at least he'd gotten Hines away from her. He'd given those damned outlaws something to think about and something to worry about.

The gunrunners would probably be arriving before the barn fire was completely out and it was sure to make them wonder if everything was all right.

Furiously, Pew yelled, 'All right, let the damn thing burn!' stopping a man who was heading in the door with a bucket of water.

There was a moment's silence, and then Pew asked angrily, 'Who the hell started it?' He looked straight at Hines. 'You was out here and so was Quigley. You must've got that damn dry manure to smoldering and it took this long for the thing to break into flame.'

Hines said, 'I wasn't smokin'. I don't know about Quigley, but I wasn't.' Pew looked at Quigley. Quigley said, 'Neither was I. But Hines got the woman cornered back there by that pile of hay. He put the lantern down on the floor. It must've happened then.'

Pew moved three steps to where Hines was standing. His fist lashed out, smashing squarely into Hines's mouth. The man staggered backward, sat down, and raised a hand to his bleeding mouth. His other hand went to the gun at his side, but Pew's rifle was already covering him. Pew said, 'Go ahead, you dumb bastard. Pull your gun. I'd like nothin' better than an excuse to blow out your stupid brains!'

Sam discovered that he was grinning.

Starting the fire had worked better than he had dared to hope it might. He had gotten Hines smashed in the mouth, something he had been itching to do himself all night. He had sowed the seeds of dissension among the outlaws. Hines wasn't the kind to forget this kind of humiliation quickly even if it did come from Pew.

By now, the fire was so hot that the outlaws had to withdraw. When it broke through the roof it lighted a huge area that reached all the way to where Sam had hidden himself.

Ramirez dragged Garcia's body away from the fire. Pew said, 'Drag him over to the creek and push him over the bank. I don't want him where he can be seen.'

Ramirez hesitated as if he would refuse. Then, apparently realizing it would only make more trouble for him if he did, he obediently dragged Garcia's body to the cutbank and, climbing into it, lifted it down carefully. Pew remained a hundred yards or so behind, not letting Ramirez get too far beyond his range.

Sam called in a whisper, 'Pedro!'

Ramirez whirled. Sam said, 'It's Sam Chance. But don't even let Lily know I'm here. Maybe I'll get a chance to do something and if I do, you be ready to help. But for God's sake, don't act any different or they'll suspect something.'

Ramirez did not reply. He only nodded his head and climbed back up out of the bed of the creek. Without looking back, he headed for the group, watching the burning barn.

CHAPTER EIGHT

Lily watched Ramirez as he climbed back out of the creek bed. He did not look at her as he returned to the group, nor did he look at Jimmy. Yet somehow, she knew something had changed; something was different.

Trying to analyze that feeling, which she admitted had no basis in fact, she began to think of the barn fire. It had begun at a time when Hines was moving closer and closer to her, whispering obscenities into her ear, when he had just laid a demanding hand upon her thigh.

Why had the fire started at such a fortuitous time? And how had it started? Neither Hines nor Quigley had smoked while they were in the barn with her. And she didn't see how the lantern could have started a fire. It had not overturned, or if it had, she hadn't seen it do so. So, despite the fact that Pew had readily blamed Hines and Quigley, and the fact that Quigley had turned the blame on Hines, she wasn't convinced that either man had started the fire. But if they had not, who had?

The answer was immediately obvious to her. Sam Chance was out there in the darkness somewhere. He knew he had no chance against the six desperadoes that held the house, held her and Jimmy and Ramirez captive and who had killed Garcia. But he was there, waiting for a chance to do something that would count.

She felt her expression brighten, and immediately controlled it before any of the outlaws could see the change. She glanced at Ramirez, but he was not looking at her. Mexican he was, but his heritage was strongly Indian, and his face was as impassive as it always was.

She wondered if Sam had been there when Hines was pawing her, when he was threatening to rip the clothes from her. Perhaps he had. But thank God he had restrained himself, however hard that must have been. Because if he had shot Hines then, the others would simply have used her, Jimmy, and Ramirez as hostages, threatening torture, rape, or death unless he immediately surrendered himself. And if he had done so, he would now either be dead, or a prisoner, as helpless as the three of them.

The barn sent up a towering column of sparks as the roof collapsed. The flames still shot twenty feet into the air, and the only thing that was not burning were the adobe walls. The door was gone, and so were the window frames.

She wondered what Sam Chance would do now. Would he return to town and raise a posse to come out here and fight these murderers? Imperceptibly she shook her head.

Pew sent Chisum back up the hill to his sentry post and ordered Quigley up the lane, instructing him to continue along the road until the fire was out of sight. He was to wait there, and as soon as the column of wagons came along, to return at a hard gallop and let Pew know. Pew would then have time to set things up so that they would look normal, despite the burning barn. Lily would say anything he told her to so long as he held Jimmy hostage, threatening to harm him if she did not.

Quigley disappeared into the darkness. Lily thought of telling the gunrunners, when they came, of the six waiting out in the darkness to murder and rob them after the guns were turned over to Villa and the money turned over to the gunrunners. Perhaps they could work something out with Villa's troops to attack the outlaw band. Yet even as she had the thought, she knew it wouldn't work. Once attacked, the outlaws would kill Jimmy first. It was a chance she simply did not dare to take.

The outlaws' horses, now in the corral, were still excited, galloping around in a circle every time smoke from the burning barn blew toward them on the breeze. Lily wondered what time it was. She guessed it must be at least three in the morning. She also guessed that the wagons containing the guns would be arriving before dawn. Villa and his troops would undoubtedly wait until it was light before they rode in. Villa was too experienced a soldier to take his troops into an unknown situation in the dark.

Finally, when the barn had burned itself out to a bed of glowing coals, Pew said, 'Come on back to the house, all of you. Quigley or Brunner will let us know in time to set things up before the gunrunners arrive.'

The three remaining outlaws herded Lily, Jimmy, and Ramirez back to the house. Lily resisted her impulse to look back in the hope that she might catch a glimpse of Sam.

Thank God for Sam, she thought. And yet, what was Sam going to think when she told him she had worked in a San Antonio saloon? Would he stand by her, or would he abandon her?

She remembered his face, his calm, steady eyes, his strong, firm mouth. She remembered his size and his strength, and she knew now, too late, that she should not have refused to marry him before her husband had been dead a year. That was a silly convention anyway. Marrying sooner implied nothing. Only that she was lonely and that someone wanted her. And being wanted the way Sam wanted her had to give any woman a feeling of warmth inside.

Sam wasn't a prude, she thought, and he certainly wasn't a saint. He was still single, which meant he'd had his share of women, saloon women and others. Furthermore, she had never heard him condemn anyone, for anything. Then why was she so afraid? Why did she think he was going to condemn her? She had been a saloon girl. But that had been six years ago. Since then, she had been a faithful wife, a good mother.

She followed Jimmy into the house. Ramirez came in behind her. The outlaws came in last, slamming the door behind. There were only three outlaws here now, and she wondered, for a moment, if Sam might not try bursting in and killing the three before they could kill him.

She decided that he would not. Sam was tough, and good with the gun he carried, but so were the outlaws inside the house. They'd be shooting back at him. And one of them would most certainly seize either Jimmy or her, threatening them if Sam did not throw down his gun.

No. Sam might have gone up against the three outlaws if the only ones involved were them and him, but under these circumstances he wouldn't take the chance.

She looked around for a place where Hines couldn't follow her. Pew didn't seem anxious for her to put Jimmy back to bed. Just the opposite. He said, 'Keep that kid in here. We may be taking him out of here any time.'

She could feel Hines's stare on her, but she tried to ignore it. Standing beside Jimmy, she tried to project her thoughts to Sam out there somewhere in the darkness. She tried to tell him that she was all right so far and not to do anything foolish just because of her. She knew, of course, that he would not receive the message of her thoughts, but just trying to send it to him made her feel safer and more secure.

But what if she had been wrong about Sam being out there somewhere? Ramirez had not even looked at her as he climbed out of the creek bed after lifting Garcia's body in. She had nothing concrete upon which to base her feeling that Sam was here.

But even though she told herself these things, she didn't doubt. Perhaps, she thought, Sam had somehow sent his thoughts to her. And maybe hers would get through to him.

Lily took Jimmy over by the kitchen stove, where she sat him down on a chair. He was sleepy and silent and docile. She lifted the lids off the stove and added a few more sticks of wood.

She realized that she was listening intently. Perhaps for some sound that Sam might make. Or perhaps for the galloping hoofs of Quigley, coming back to tell Pew that the wagons were on their way.

*   *   *

Time dragged for Sam, standing well back from the house now because of the glow

70

thrown over the entire yard by the breeze-fanned embers of the burned-out barn. He couldn't see what was going on in the kitchen; he was too far away. But he could occasionally see a figure moving across from one side of it to the other.

Three men were in the house. One was up on the hill behind the house, a position he had resumed after the fire had died down. Both Quigley and Joe Brunner were up the road, waiting for the wagons to show up.

Sam couldn't see his watch; there was not enough light for it. But he had looked at in the fire's light back in the creek bed and it had been three-ten then. It must be close to four by now. Before long, dawn would begin showing as a line of gray in the eastern sky and soon afterward the whole sky would begin turning gray. By five he would have to find some place to hide himself and his horse and by five-thirty it would be light enough to see for half a mile.

What Pew intended to do if the wagons showed up before dawn, Sam had no idea. How would Lily and Ramirez explain to the gunrunners that they were up so long before dawn? Maybe Pew hadn't thought of that. Or maybe he was sure enough that the wagons wouldn't arrive before dawn that he hadn't really considered it.

There was also a chance that Villa, wary in this hostile land, would fan out scouts and skirmishers as he approached and would

71

discover Joe Brunner, Quigley, and Les. If that happened, Villa would kill the three as unhesitatingly as he would exterminate a nest of mice, and after that the three outlaws in the house. But would that improve Lily's chances to survive.

Dillman and his gunrunners were another complication. They wouldn't want to leave witnesses behind to give descriptions of them to the authorities any more than the outlaws did. Still, Sam Chance realized that he had a better chance with the gunrunners than he did against Pew and his men. He *knew* Pew intended to kill Lily and her son. The gunrunners might conceivably be a different breed.

So he waited, and at last saw a faint line of gray outline the horizon in the east. He began to look around for a place to hide, and he headed for his horse, still standing tied several hundred yards away.

CHAPTER NINE

Dillman, riding at the head of the slow-moving column of wagons, knew they had to be getting fairly close to their destination. He had never been to the place before, but it had been carefully described to him by Villa's emissary, with whom the gun sale had been arranged. It was built of adobe, contained but two rooms, and had an adobe barn with a large hayloft. He knew there were several other, smaller buildings, an adobe icehouse, a chicken house, and a root cellar dug into the ground and covered heavily with sod. There was also a corral and, beyond the buildings, there was a creek that seldom ran more than a trickle, but which the occupants of the ranch used for stock and domestic water, and sometimes, when there was enough of it, for irrigating their garden crops.

A man named MacDonald had owned the ranch until he was killed nearly a year ago when a horse fell on him. Now the place was run by his widow, who had a small son, and by two Mexican cowboys.

A vague, pervasive feeling of uneasiness was still troubling Dillman and he was at a loss to account for it. Ernst had dropped behind and now rode beside one of the wagons about halfway back. As Dillman stared back that way, both Ernst and the wagon stopped. Ernst then dismounted, tied his horse to the tail gate, and climbed up onto the wagon seat. Ernst's buttocks and thighs were too sore for any more saddle riding, thought Dillman, but he had better get them to feeling better before tomorrow. Tomorrow they'd be on their way out of this part of the country and Ernst would have to ride and ride hard with the rest of them.

He began to think of the occupants of the

ranch where the exchange was going to take place. A woman. A boy. Two Mexicans. The Mexicans were probably sympathetic toward Villa, and if they were, would pose no threat. The woman could be frightened sufficiently to make her forget what any of Dillman's men had looked like. There needn't be any violence and Dillman wanted none. It was one thing to sell rifles to a Mexican revolutionary, even stolen ones. That, while it was against the law, was being done every day and seldom was anybody prosecuted for doing it. Killing was something else and he wanted no part of it.

But the feeling of uneasiness continued. Dillman began trying to rationalize it. Obviously, the woman, the boy, and the two Mexicans who lived at the ranch posed no threat to his own heavily armed men, even if he discounted Ernst.

So his uneasiness could not be caused by worry over the inhabitants of the ranch. Villa, then. Maybe Villa didn't mean to buy the rifles at all. Maybe he meant to take them by force, killing the sellers down to the last man. But that would mean killing the woman, the boy, and the two Mexicans because they were witnesses. That much killing would create an international incident and bring the United States Government, already exasperated with Villa, down hard on the Mexican Government for failing to curb the outlaws' excesses. It could even lead to war.

That Villa would kill them then, did not seem likely. Villa had enough money to buy the rifles, even at a cost of a hundred thousand dollars. He looted the banks of every town he occupied. He levied stiff taxes against the rich landowners when he wasn't expropriating their property to distribute among the poor.

Unless Villa *wanted* to create an international incident. Dillman knew, from reading the newspapers, how jealous the various revolutionary commanders in Mexico were of each other. Carranza, the First Chief, would like nothing better than to be rid of Villa for good. And Villa probably felt the same way about Carranza, who would have had him arrested and shot if he had been able to manage it.

Dillman suddenly made up his mind. Along with the rifles, he had three machine guns, and plenty of ammunition for them. He raised a hand and bellowed at the column to halt. Then, riding back, he halted beside each of three wagons. He said, 'I want you to get one of those machine guns and mount it right beside you on the seat. Keep ammunition for it on the floorboards so you can get to it easily.'

Gwin asked, 'What's the matter, you think Villa might try to take the guns without paying for them?'

'The thought has occurred to me. Go ahead and do what I said. Light lanterns if you have to and everybody pitch in. That Mexican

75

bandit isn't going to get a damn thing until I see the color of his money. But if we have to shoot it out with him, then we need these machine guns to even things up.'

The men climbed down from the halted wagons, dragged the heavy machine guns out from underneath the canvas. Laboriously, and by lantern light, they mounted the guns on the wagon seats next to the driver's seat with whatever screws and bolts they were able to find in the toolboxes carried on each wagon. In three quarters of an hour the job was done. Dillman said, 'Feed a belt into each one of them and jack a cartridge into the chamber. I want them ready to fire the instant I give the word.'

He heard the sounds of the belts being put into place, the sounds of the guns' actions being worked to insert the first cartridge of each belt into the chamber of each gun. He yelled, 'All right. Let's go!'

He rode to the head of the column again, and the wagons rumbled into motion behind him. Dillman thought that now, after having taken every precaution he could, his feeling of uneasiness ought to have decreased. But it had not.

Finally he simply shrugged it away, telling himself that for big profits you have to take big risks.

It was still half an hour before dawn when Dillman thought he saw a glow in the sky ahead and to his left, where the ranch should be. He watched for several minutes, saw nothing further. Shortly thereafter, he thought he heard the sound of galloping hoofs ahead of him but they too subsided. The wagons behind him, and his own horse, were making too much noise to hear anything else at any distance.

Jumpy and wary, he went on, as dawn began to lighten the eastern sky. He'd have secured the ranch house by the time Villa arrived, he thought. Villa was too smart a commander to ride into an unknown situation in the dark, and he probably wouldn't show up until sunrise.

He'd be ready, with his machine guns and his heavily armed crew, and he'd have the protection of the ranch buildings, too. If Villa meant to betray him, there were going to be a lot of dead bodies lying around that ranch yard before this was over with.

*   *   *

There was a streak of gray in the eastern sky when Joe Brunner and Quigley came galloping into the yard. They immediately unsaddled and turned their horses loose. Sweaty horses inside the corral were sure to attract the attention of the gunrunners when they arrived. With shouts and waving of their arms, they chased the horses down into the brushy creek bottom where they would be out of sight.

Their saddles, blankets, and bridles they

77

carried to the root cellar, and heaved them down inside. They also got two of the four saddles from the corral fence where their comrades had left them earlier, and tossed them into the root cellar after their own.

Les Chisum came walking down off the hill behind the house. All three went in. 'They're coming. We'd better get out of here.'

Pew gestured at Hines to go out. Al Brunner, Joe's older brother, followed him. Pew picked up Jimmy from the chair beside the stove, holding him with an arm around the child's middle. Jimmy began to scream and kick and Pew said harshly, 'Lady, you'd better tell him to shut up or I'll shut him up.'

Lily came close to Jimmy, her eyes bright with tears. She knew this might be the last time she ever saw her son alive, and yet there was nothing on earth she could do to change anything. At least not now.

She said, 'Jimmy.'

He only screamed louder. In a firmer and louder tone she said sharply, 'Jimmy!'

He stopped crying briefly.

Lily said, 'Everything is going to be all right and they're not going to hurt you as long as you don't make any noise.'

His big, tear-filled eyes stared at her with so much trust that she felt ashamed. She didn't know that what she'd told him was true. She could only hope. Still firmly she said, 'No more crying now. They'll hit you if you do.'

He didn't cry, but the trust in his eyes changed to fear. All the way out the door, his eyes clung to hers and it was all she could do to keep from screaming and running after him.

Then the door closed and she and Pedro Ramirez were left alone inside the house. One last time the door opened and Pew stuck his head inside. 'You two had better make it good. Just keep thinking about that kid. The first sign we get that something's wrong and he breathes his last.'

She had no time to reply. The door slammed. With tears brimming from her eyes and running across her cheeks, she asked in a trembling voice, 'Oh, Pedro! What are we going to do?' She ran to the front window and stared out, in time to see Pew, carrying Jimmy, disappear around the corner of the house.

Pedro was silent until she looked at him. Then, apparently unable to stand the sight of her grief any longer, he said, 'He told me not to tell you, but señora, I cannot watch you grieve this way. Sam Chance is out there somewhere. He will help us if he can.'

Lily dabbed at her eyes with a handkerchief. 'I don't know how I knew it, but I guessed he was here. But what can *he* do? What can any one man do? There are six of them and more coming.'

'If we do what they say ...'

She shook her head. 'It isn't going to make one bit of difference what we do. They have already killed Heraldo. They will kill again before they get the money that Villa is going to pay those other men for the guns. Do you think they will leave anyone alive to testify against them and put a hangman's noose around their necks?'

'Something may happen.'

She nodded hopelessly. But she didn't believe it and the fact that she did not showed plainly in her eyes.

She was only hoping that Sam wouldn't do anything foolish, anything that would cost him his life. But she knew Sam. She knew that when the final hour came, when the guns were raised to kill her, Pedro, and Jimmy, that he'd act. No matter how foolish or hopeless it might be, he would do something. He wouldn't just stand by and watch them killed even if letting his presence be known meant his own certain death.

For an instant it gave her a warm feeling to know that Sam cared that much for her. Then the cold of fear returned.

It was gray dawn outside the house by now. She stared up the lane leading to the road, waiting for the wagons to come into sight. A light fog lay over the land and she could not see very far through it. But there was a pink glow in the eastern sky and she knew that as soon as the sun came up it would burn off the fog.

Ramirez said, 'Señora?'

'What?'

'These men who are coming with the guns. Maybe they are not as bad as the ones who are here now. Maybe if you tell them what the others have done, if you warn them of what they intend to do, they will be grateful enough to save Jimmy for you.'

Lily shook her head. 'They are lawbreakers just the same as the ones who have Jimmy. Why should they take any risks just to save one little boy? No, they would attack these men who have Jimmy and he would be killed, either by the ones who have him now or the ones who are bringing the guns.'

'Then how about Pancho Villa? I have heard that he is a good man and will help people like us whenever he can.'

Lily shook her head. 'I'm afraid you have heard wrong, Pedro. I have heard he is a man who makes his prisoners stand four in line so that he may kill four with each bullet.'

'Then what are we to do, señora?'

'Nothing for now, I guess. We'll just have to wait and see what happens. Sam is out there someplace and he will save Jimmy if he can.'

She could now see Spot, lying where they had left him when they carried him out of the burning barn. He was lying still, but suddenly he raised his head and stared up the lane toward the road.

He had heard the wagons, Lily thought, and they ought to be coming into sight pretty soon. She said, 'They're coming.'

Spot began to bark. And then, dimly through the dissipating fog, Lily saw a single horseman ride into view. He carried a rifle in a saddle boot but he carried a double-barreled shotgun across the saddle in front of him. He rode warily, looking to right and left and trying to penetrate the fog so that he could look beyond the house.

Not long afterward, she saw the first wagon, with its double teams, come into sight. It was loaded only a little higher than the sideboards and had a heavy canvas cover over it. The canvas was tightly lashed down with rope.

Something beside the driver caught her eye. She had never seen a machine gun before but she knew instinctively what it was.

These men, she thought, had come heavily armed and prepared. And a little more of her hope for Jimmy's life faded.

She clenched her jaw. Now was the time when she would need every bit of strength she possessed. When those men came in here, she had to make them believe there was nothing wrong. Otherwise, Jimmy didn't have any chance at all.

CHAPTER TEN

Pew, Hines, Les Chisum, the Brunner brothers, and Del Quigley took up a position behind the low, adobe icehouse. Pew still held Jimmy beneath his left arm, effortlessly because Pew was very strong and Jimmy very light. Jimmy was quiet, scared into silence. Pew peered around the corner of the icehouse, watching the lane, trying to penetrate the light fog and catch a glimpse of the wagons coming toward him.

Quigley asked, 'Hadn't we better get clear back out of sight? We don't want 'em to know we're here until after the exchange has taken place.'

Pew frowned. 'All right. But I don't want to be bottled up. Let's back away and watch from down in the bed of the creek.'

Immediately the men left the icehouse, keeping it between them and the lane, and retreated to the bank of the narrow stream. The bank here was about four feet high. They couldn't stand and watch, but they could stay out of sight and there was enough high grass along the creek so that one man could watch without being seen.

Pew handed Jimmy to Quigley. 'Don't let him yell and don't let him get away. Knock him out if that's what it takes to keep him still.'

The outlaw leader raised his head cautiously and peered through the high grass and up the lane. He saw a single horseman come into sight. The man had his horse at a slow and steady walk and he kept looking warily to right and left, as though he expected an ambush.

Pew glanced at Joe Brunner. 'You sure they didn't see or hear you?'

'I don't see how. They couldn't have seen us because we never even saw them. And I don't see how they could've heard us with all the racket them wagons were making.'

Pew nodded, reassured. It was probably just that the gunrunners didn't trust Pancho Villa. And with good reason, he thought. Villa needed guns for his army and if he couldn't get them one way, he'd get them another.

Behind the horseman, a wagon appeared, drawn by two teams. Pew saw something on the wagon seat beside the driver and narrowed his eyes, trying to make out what it was. Finally he breathed, 'Those sonsabitches have got machine guns mounted on the wagon seats!'

Beside him, Del Quigley shrugged. 'So what? They just don't trust Villa, that's all. Villa will take the machine guns along with the rifles when he leaves. All we'll have to worry about will be ordinary guns. Besides, we'll take them by surprise.'

The wagons were now in view, all six of them. They drew up in a line in front of the house. Pew now saw that only three of the six wagons had machine guns mounted on their seats. He also noticed that the drivers of those three wagons stayed on the seats beside their guns, swinging the muzzles around so that the guns covered the house and outbuildings.

The horseman, who had been riding in the

84

lead, got down and went first to the dog, lying on his side, barking as furiously as he could. The man spoke to the dog and, a few moments later, knelt and petted him on the head. Briefly his hands explored the dog's body for his injury. When he touched the dog's injured side, the animal yelped.

Pew muttered, 'Damn! We should've gotten rid of that dog! He knows the dog's been kicked. But maybe he'll think he was kicked by a horse.'

The rider straightened from the dog and glanced warily around once more at the house and at all the outbuildings, including the still glowing embers of the burned-out barn. He kept his shotgun cradled in his arms, ready to raise it and fire the minute anything threatening appeared.

To himself, Pew muttered, 'Lady, if you value your kid, you'd better get on out of that house. I told you to make it look natural.'

As if she had heard him, Lily MacDonald opened the door of the house and came out, followed by Ramirez. The man with the shotgun turned and walked toward the woman and the Mexican.

He raised a hand and touched the brim of his hat. 'Morning, ma'am.' His voice carried well in the clear morning air and thinning fog.

She nodded, then turned her head to look at the line of wagons and waiting men. She asked, 'What do you want? What are you doing here?'

85

'We've got six wagonloads of guns and ammunition for Pancho Villa. He's going to come for them sometime today. In the meantime, ma'am, I'm going to have to ask you and your boy and your two cowhands to stay in the house.'

She nodded numbly. Pew asked harshly beneath his breath, 'How the hell did they know about the kid and that other Mexican?'

Quigley said, 'You don't think Pancho Villa is going to ride in anyplace without knowing what's there, do you? Villa likely told them.'

Lily turned and went back into the house. Ramirez followed her. The man who had spoken to her walked over and stared at the embers of the barn. He was not able to get closer than twenty-five or thirty feet because of the heat. Having inspected the ruins, he walked to the house, disappearing behind the corner of it. Pew heard him knocking on the door but he couldn't hear anything that was said because of the intervening adobe walls of the house.

He supposed the man was asking what had happened to start the fire in the barn. After several minutes, the man appeared and beckoned the drivers of the three wagons which did not have machine guns mounted on them. Pew heard him say, 'There's something fishy here. She says her kid is in town with his grandparents. She says the other Mexican is out fixing fence, that he left first thing this morning. Look around and see what kind of tracks you can pick out of all this mess.'

'You think Villa's already here?' one of the men said as he looked uneasily toward the creek.

The first man shook his head. 'I don't know what I think. But Villa wouldn't ride in here in the dark. He's got too much sense for that.'

All four men began working the yard, studying the ground for tracks. Pew cursed softly under his breath.

He didn't know what the men found, but he knew there were a lot of tracks in the yard, more than anyone would normally expect in a sleepy little place like this. Finally the man stopped the search. He then ordered the horses in the corral turned out. He had six of their eight saddle horses put inside. The horses belonging to Pew and his men wandered down into the creek bottom where, presumably, there was feed and water for them.

Pew spoke to Quigley and Joe Brunner. 'Go catch one of them. Bring him back here and tie him up.'

Quigley and Brunner walked away in the direction the horses had gone. One horse would be enough, Pew thought, to keep tied up. With him, they could always round up the others and drive them back into the corral. After Villa had paid for and departed with the guns and before the gunrunners had a chance to leave.

*　　*　　*

Lily didn't really know whether she had put on a convincing performance a few moments before or not. She had no way of knowing what her expression had shown the man out in the yard. Some puzzlement would be natural since she would be wondering about the sudden appearance of six heavily loaded wagons and eight heavily armed men.

The story about Jimmy being in town with grandparents had come to her tongue after only a moment's groping. She had been surprised that the man knew exactly who should have been here. But he had seemed to accept the story about Jimmy along with the one she'd told about Garcia being out mending fence.

Now she peered out the window and watched four of them covering the yard, studying it for tracks. They continued to prowl the yard for ten or fifteen minutes. Then they conferred briefly, probably about what they had found—more tracks than would normally be present in an isolated ranch yard like this one.

The one who had ridden down the lane first, and who seemed to be in charge, had his own horse. Another saddled horse had been tied to a wagon about halfway back in the column and six other horses had been put into the corral after first turning out the horses already there.

These were the eight horses, she thought, on which they meant to make their getaway.

Fourteen men, she thought bleakly. Six in hiding beyond the ranch house grounds who were committed to killing her, Ramirez, and Jimmy before they left. Eight more in the yard, armed with three machine guns in addition to the arms they carried, who also would want no witnesses left behind who could identify them to the authorities. And Villa coming, probably with at least fifty of his soldiers, men who executed without question anyone Villa ordered them to kill.

She could face death herself, she thought. She could face it, even though she didn't want to die any more than anybody else. Particularly now that her marriage to Sam was so very close.

But the thought of Jimmy being killed, Jimmy who was only five years old, that thought was more than she could bear.

She walked to the window and stared at the machine guns on the wagons outside in the yard. She felt the faintest touch of hope. Sam Chance was out there somewhere, keeping himself hidden, but waiting for his opportunity. If he could get to one of those machine guns, overpowering the man with the wagon, and then turn it on the others...

She shook her head. It wouldn't help Jimmy, in the hands of the six hidden outlaws.

Ramirez said, 'Señora, I am sorry. I am here

not only to work for you but to protect you too. And I have not done so.'

She turned her head. 'I'm glad you didn't try. Heraldo tried and now he's dead. I would not want your death on my conscience too.'

'Pancho Villa will be here soon.'

'How many men do you think he will bring with him?'

'It is nearly twenty miles to Mexico by road. With those heavy wagons, that will take all day. He will need enough men to fight off the United States Army if necessary. A hundred, he will bring. Or more.'

'What about those machine guns? Do you think he'll take them too? Or will the gunrunners keep them?'

'Villa will take them, señora. They are very heavy and must be mounted on something solid. On those wagons, they will be very valuable to Villa. In the hands of a horseman, they would be useless.'

'Then after Villa pays over the money, takes the guns, and leaves ... the six men who have Jimmy will simply open fire on the eight who brought the guns and slaughter them before they know what is going on?'

Ramirez nodded. 'Señora, that is the way it is going to be. And only after the fight is over and all the gunrunners killed, will you get little Jimmy back.'

Lily shook her head. 'You don't believe that, Pedro, and neither do I. The men who have

Jimmy are not going to leave any of us alive.'

The sun was up now, and had burned off most of the morning fog. Lily thought that Villa would be coming soon. And she was helpless. So was Sam. As long as the outlaws held Jimmy hostage, there was nothing any of them could do.

Nothing but wait. And hope. And pray that somehow God could alter the apparently inevitable course of events.

CHAPTER ELEVEN

From the bend of the creek several hundred yards upstream from Pew and his men, Sam Chance watched the arrival of the gunrunners, led by one solitary horseman. As they materialized out of the light morning fog, he saw that three of the six wagons had machine guns mounted on their seats. They must have been recently mounted, he thought, since the gunrunners would not dare display them openly along their route. They must have been mounted and readied because the gunrunners expected some kind of treachery from the Mexican revolutionary.

Sam knew Pew had Jimmy. He had seen the terrified child carried away. Lily and Pedro Ramirez were inside the house. Now they had come out, and Lily talked briefly with the leader of the gunrunners but because of the distance he couldn't hear what was being said.

The man who had led the gunrunners down the lane now walked toward the still hot and smoldering embers of the barn and stood there for a moment staring at them.

Sam couldn't tell whether he suspected something or not. He must have, though, because immediately afterward he called some of his men to him and they all began to prowl the yard, studying the tracks.

There were too many fresh tracks, far too many, for a sleepy little place like this. The man was certain to notice that and he might try to pry more information out of Lily. Sam had no way of knowing what he might do to her if she didn't talk.

As sheriff of this county, Sam would be within his rights to open fire. Considering they had machine guns, he'd be justified in killing without mercy.

It would be difficult, though, if not impossible to get them all unless he could reach one of the machine guns and turn it on them.

In any case, things seemed to have stabilized, at least temporarily. Lily and Ramirez were probably safe until Villa arrived. Jimmy, being held by Pew, was surely terrified, but he was in no immediate danger of being hurt or killed. Pew needed him, and knew he'd get no cooperation out of Lily if anything happened to the boy.

Sam tried to remember all he had heard about Pancho Villa because upon what Villa did was going to depend the outcome of this.

He knew Villa had begun with only a handful of revolutionaries, less than a dozen as a matter of fact, and had lost half of them in his first fight. But Villa was a colorful figure, somehow capable of attracting men to him, of inspiring and holding their loyalty.

When captured *rurales* or federal troops were brought before him he was as likely to say simply, 'Shoot them,' as he was to let them change sides and join the forces of the revolution.

Now this savage, unpredictable man was coming here. Perhaps with fifty men, perhaps with many more. Sam knew he might simply take the guns and kill the men who had brought them here. Or he might pay, in good faith, take the guns, and go. But if he learned of Pew's presence, then all hell was likely to break loose. Pew and his five men would provide the spark and set off a conflagration. Believing himself betrayed, Villa would open fire and ask questions afterward.

Another thing troubled Sam. Pew had only five men, with himself making six. The gunrunners were eight in all. Under ordinary circumstances, the gunrunners had the better chance. Sam doubted if Pew's possession of Jimmy as a hostage would make any difference to the gunrunners if they were faced with the loss of the money they had been paid for the guns.

Pew, then, must be counting on killing them from ambush, simply opening fire when the gunrunners were least expecting it, probably when they broke open the money chests to gloat over their loot.

In the meantime, all he could do was wait. Maybe in the confusion, he'd be able to get Jimmy, Lily, and Ramirez away. Maybe he could get to Villa and make him believe that Pew and his men were U.S. customs officers. If he could rescue Jimmy first.

Too many ifs, he thought. Too little chance. But he had no choice. If the lives of Jimmy, Lily, and Ramirez were to be saved, he was the one who would have to save them. If the job turned out to be too big for him, then all of them were going to die.

*   *   *

Dillman didn't like the number of fresh horse tracks in the yard of this small and isolated ranch. He didn't see how they could have been made, unless a number of men were already here, hidden, waiting for the gun exchange to take place.

Dillman stopped and glanced toward the bed of the creek. Fifty men could hide down there, he thought. But who were they? The U.S. Army? He doubted that. How could the Army have known that Villa would come here to buy guns today? U.S. customs men? Again he shook his head. They'd have made their presence known before now. They'd have confiscated the wagons, arrested the gunrunners, and let Villa go empty-handed back to Mexico.

Who, then? He called his men together and led them over behind one of of the wagons, one which had a machine gun mounted on its seat. He said, 'Too many horses. What do you make of it?'

One man said, 'Army?'

Dillman shook his head. 'Neither the Army nor the customs men would have stayed out of sight this long. They'd have come out and confiscated the guns. Huh uh, it's got to be somebody else.'

'Maybe somebody followed us.'

Dillman stared at Hibbert. 'Maybe somebody got drunk and blabbed.'

'What the hell are you looking at me for?' Hibbert asked defensively. 'I didn't say nothing about the guns.'

'What did you say something about?'

Hibbert scowled. 'Well hell, maybe I said something about having a lot of money pretty soon. But nothing more than that.'

Disgustedly Dillman said, 'You dumb sonofabitch! Before I came for you, you must have blabbed enough to make somebody wonder what you were talking about. I'll bet they trailed us. They saw these wagons and guessed from the way they were loaded what was in them.'

One of the other men, Gwin, said, 'Huh uh. Nobody pays any attention to what a drunk brags about.'

Dillman stared at him. 'Then how do *you* explain it?'

'I don't see what we've got to worry about. There's eight of us. Villa may take the machine guns, but we've all got both hand guns and rifles. You've even got a shotgun. It'd take a hell of a lot of men to get that money away from us.'

Dillman's worried expression seemed to relax. Gwin said, 'Why don't you put a little pressure on that woman? Make her tell you if anybody's here.'

Dillman shook his head. He was thinking that if somebody was here, they had probably taken the little boy as a hostage to be sure the woman said what they told her to. Following that logic a bit further, he guessed that the other Mexican probably was a captive too. Or dead. Those two assumptions would explain the way the woman had acted, so extremely nervous and evasive.

The chances were good, he thought, that whoever was out there wouldn't do anything at least until Villa had taken possession of the guns. They certainly would have no desire to go up against the three machine guns mounted

96

on the wagon seats. It was only after the money had been paid for the guns and Villa had departed that they would become dangerous.

Dillman didn't know how many of them there were. What he did know was that when they struck it would be swiftly and unexpectedly, counting on the element of surprise.

But there would be no surprise. Dillman and his men, expecting the attack, would be ready for it. And they would slaughter the ones who meant to rob them of the money they had been paid for the guns.

* * *

The sun was well up in the sky, and had burned off the last of the early-morning fog before Pancho Villa and his men rode up the slope of a low rise, from the top of which they could see the MacDonald ranch. Villa smiled when he saw the six wagons down below. He frowned slightly when he saw that three of them had machine guns mounted on the wagon seats and that a man was standing by each gun.

He stared down uncertainly. Why the machine guns? And why were they manned? Did Dillman expect an attack by the United States Army? Puzzledly, Villa shook his head. But neither did it seem likely that Dillman meant to turn the guns on him. Dillman had six wagon-loads of guns and ammunition that he wanted to sell. He had no way of knowing Villa had packaged worthless pesos with U.S. dollars on the outside.

Having decided that, the faint smile returned to Villa's face. He would be glad to get the machine guns, which certainly would go with the deal for the simple reason that the gringo gunrunners couldn't carry them back on the saddles of their horses. Furthermore, he thought, the machine guns would make quick work of Dillman and his men once the deal had been consummated and he had taken possession of the weapons.

But still he sat, studying the land before him. A thin plume of smoke came from the chimney of the house. Dillman's men lounged near the wagons, four of them playing cards. Dillman himself stood nearby, not seeming to look around but doing it nevertheless.

There was a dog lying between the wagons and the still smoking remains of what once had probably been a barn. The fire must have been last night, and that puzzled Villa too.

His glance went on. There were six horses in the corral and two more tied to the wagons, saddle horses, the ones the gunrunners meant to use when they left. Down in the creek bottom, Villa could see several more horses and guessed that these must be the ones belonging to the people who owned the ranch.

Something else suddenly caught Villa's eye. It was right at the edge of the creek next to the cutbank and was so vague that at first he believed he had imagined it. But, fixing his eyes upon that spot, he saw it again. It was a bluish wisp of smoke. Someone was down there, hiding, and he had been foolish enough to light a pipe.

Villa continued to sit while the horses of the men lowered their heads and began to graze. Maybe, thought Villa, Dillman had found out about the state bank he had established and about the printing presses that were working twenty-four hours a day. Maybe Dillman suspected he was going to be paid for the guns with this worthless currency. That would explain the machine guns. It would also explain men hidden down in the bed of the creek.

Villa glanced back at the men he had brought with him. They wore no regular uniforms. Instead, most of them were dressed like any *campesino* of northern Mexico. Many wore sandals. All had cotton pants. Some wore shirts taken from dead *Rurales*, and all wore the wide-brimmed straw hats so universally popular in Chihuahua and Sonora, farther to the west.

Most were unshaven, and the hair of many of them was long for the simple reason that they seldom saw a barber or had a chance to get it cut. Some wore mustaches but none wore beards.

A gringo might have said they were a

villainous-looking lot. Villa smiled at the thought. They were only as villainous as their leader, for they obeyed his every command, no matter what it was.

And was he villainous, Villa asked himself with wry amusement? Well, Carranza thought he was. Huerta thought he was. Madero had thought he was a man of excesses and had at one time even imprisoned him. But Madero had never doubted his loyalty. Now, even with Madero dead, Villa remained loyal to the principles for which Madero had stood: Freedom and justice for all. A fair distribution of both land and wealth.

Staring at the spot from which the smoke had come, Villa caught the movement of a clump of brush. A moment later, he briefly saw the head of a man and, a few moments later, the head of another one.

He wondered how many men Dillman had concealed down there. He doubted if there could be more than a dozen or so. Add to that the eight in the yard and you still had less than twenty men. Villa himself had seventy-five.

Would the machine guns open up on them the instant he and his men rode into the yard? He shrugged his ponderous shoulders faintly. He didn't think so but they would find out. In a few minutes, they were going to find out.

CHAPTER TWELVE

Dillman did not see Villa and his men for the simple reason that they were mostly hidden from sight behind the hill. Only the heads of Villa and two or three of his men showed above its crest.

Suddenly, aware that Villa would be here very soon, but also certain that another group of men were concealed in the creek bottom, Dillman turned away from the wagons and strode swiftly to the house. For his own safety and that of his men, he had to know how many men were waiting in the creek bottom, what their intentions were, and, if possible, when they planned to strike.

He entered without knocking. The Mexican cowboy was standing at the window looking out. He turned toward the door as it opened, but he made no other movement.

The woman was at the stove. She had one of the stove lids off and was adding wood to the fire. Her head turned quickly, fearfully, at the sound of the door.

Dillman closed it behind him. He stood there silently for several moments. Staring toward the fireplace, he saw what was left of the rifle now for the first time. He also noticed the pegs in the wall where the rifle had hung. He saw a few toys in the corner of the room.

He crossed the room, studying the floor, the walls, the furniture, missing nothing. Near the fireplace, he saw bloodstains on the floor. He turned his head. Looking straight at Lily, he said, 'You lied to me, didn't you? They killed your other cowhand and they've kidnaped your boy. They're holding him so that you'll do what they tell you to.'

Her face lost what little color was left in it. Her eyes looked like those of a cornered animal.

Dillman hated to frighten her this way, but he had to know the truth. Trying to calm her somewhat, he asked, 'How old is the boy?'

Her voice was no more than a whisper. 'Five.'

'And they've got him. They're probably hiding down there in the creek bottom. Aren't they?'

She shook her head. 'I told you he was in town with his grandparents.'

'You also told me your other cowhand was out fixing fence. But how do you explain that smashed rifle in the fireplace? And the bloodstains on the floor?'

She seemed unable to speak. Her eyes pleaded silently with him.

He said, 'I've got to know how many of them there are. And I've got to know something about them and what they intend to do.'

She was trembling now and he felt sorry for her. She was a pretty woman. He wondered if they had molested her last night. He insisted, 'I've got to know. But there's no way I'm going to let them know you've told me anything.'

Pedro Ramirez said, 'Tell him, señora. Perhaps he can help you get Jimmy back unhurt.'

Lily nodded uncertainly. Finally she said, 'They came last night. One of them kicked the dog. I think he has some broken ribs because it seems to hurt him too much to get up and move around.

'Then they came into the house. One of them, a big man named Hines, began pawing me. Heraldo tried to get the gun hanging on the wall. They shot him in the chest. He died instantly. Then they smashed the gun and threw it into the fireplace.'

'What about the barn? Did they burn that?'

Lily didn't intend to tell them that Sam was out there someplace. That was one thing they'd never pry out of her. So she only nodded. 'Accidentally.'

'And when they saw us coming, they took your son as a hostage to make sure you didn't tell us they were here.'

Again she nodded.

'What do they intend to do?'

'I think they're going to wait until you have sold the rifles to Francisco Villa and have the money for them. They will wait until Villa leaves. Then they will attack you and your men and try to kill you all before you realize what is happening.'

'What are some of their names?'

'Their leader is named Ezra Pew. There are two brothers named Brunner. One is Al and the other Joe. The one who killed Heraldo is Pew.'

Dillman had been staring into a box beside the stove. It had a number of broken dishes dumped into it. Curiously, Dillman asked, 'What happened to the dishes?'

For the first time the faintest of smiles touched the woman's mouth. 'I hit the one named Hines with them. I got tired of being pawed.'

'And what happened then?'

'He came for me, but I had a pan of hot dishwater ready for him. Before anything more happened, Pew stopped him by threatening to kill him.'

Dillman had crossed to the window and was now peering out. He saw Villa, a huge man who rode like he was part of his horse, picking his way down the slight rise south of the house. His men followed him, spread out, each separated by at least twenty feet from the next.

Dillman knew the scattered approach was because of the machine guns mounted on the wagon seats. Glancing at the wagons, he saw that the men manning the guns had swung the muzzles toward Villa and his men.

He said quickly, 'Thanks, ma'am. That bunch holding your son won't know from me that you've told me anything.'

She nodded, but her eyes showed doubt. Dillman didn't have time to reassure her further. He stepped out into the yard, hoping none of Villa's men would be foolish enough to try picking off one of the machine gunners, hoping too that Villa didn't have another column approaching from the other side.

He was also hoping that his own men, manning the machine guns, would be steady and not easily spooked if one of Villa's men made a gesture that looked threatening.

Behind him, Lily prayed that she had not doomed Jimmy by telling Dillman everything.

Sam Chance kept himself hidden below the cutbank at the side of the creek bottom for a long time, getting more fidgety with every passing moment. He was exceedingly nervous. Reason told him there was very little chance that Lily, or Jimmy, or Pedro, or he himself would be alive by noon. Nor was standing here accomplishing anything. Damn it, there ought to be something useful he could do!

But the only thing he could think of was to try and reduce the numbers of the men waiting hidden several hundred yards farther downstream from him and that was too dangerous as far as Jimmy was concerned.

His own horse was tied back where the willows and brush were thick and where it was unlikely he would be seen. The outlaws' horses were loose in the creek bottom, grazing peacefully, pretty much staying in one place. They had kept one horse to use in rounding up the other five and driving them back into the corral when this was over with.

Sam thought that if he could get to the outlaws' horses without being seen, he could drive them downstream and when the outlaws realized they were moving away, they would most likely send one of their number to bring them back.

Villa had not yet appeared at the crest of the knoll as Sam moved away from his hiding place. But Villa was there, only his head and the heads of two or three of his subordinates visible.

As silently as he could, Sam worked his way back through the heavy brush. He had the outlaws' position spotted, and he took care never to come closer than two hundred yards to it. What few noises he made unavoidably would probably be blamed on the grazing horses by the hidden outlaw band.

Coming close to the outlaws' horses, Sam kept himself out of sight, but he picked up a handful of small rocks and tossed them one by one toward the horses, who immediately raised their heads in alarm and curiosity. Sam threw another handful of rocks, one at a time and the horses began moving downstream, not frightened, but puzzled. They moved slowly and naturally in a way that would not arouse the suspicions of the outlaw gang.

Sam heard one of the outlaws say, 'The horses. They're moving away downstream.'

Pew said, 'They won't go far.'

Another of the outlaws said, 'Maybe not. But when we need them we're going to need them fast. We're not going to have time to look for them all over the place.'

Pew said, 'All right then. Take this horse and go after them. But don't make a lot of noise. I figure Villa is due here anytime.'

Sam heard the creak of saddle leather as the man mounted, the metallic jangle of a bit, and then the horse moving away through the brush.

Immediately he began to trot, but instead of trying to move through the brush and grass, he turned instead and sought out the sandy bottom of the near-dry stream. Here he could run fast enough to keep up with the outlaw on horseback without taking the risk of being heard.

On his left, he could hear the outlaw's horse crashing through the brush. The sounds came from slightly ahead of him.

He hoped he could overpower and kill the man without using his gun. But he realized that there was not much chance of it.

One thing lessened the danger of what he meant to do. If one of the outlaws was killed by a bullet, it would now probably be blamed on one of Villa's scouts. Maybe he had scouts out and maybe he did not, but the outlaws, when they heard the shot and found one of their number dead, would assume Villa was responsible.

Killing one would cut the odds to five.

Sam picked up his pace until he was breathing hard. He was rewarded by hearing the sound of the outlaw's horse now abreast of him.

Perhaps an eighth of a mile now separated the mounted outlaw from the other five keeping themselves hidden below the cutbank at the edge of the stream bed. He could move in now, Sam Chance thought.

He left the sandy bed of the nearly dry stream and took to the grass and brush at the side of it. There was an exhilaration in him now. No longer was he completely helpless. No longer must he stand by and watch events move to their inevitable, deadly climax. Here was something he could do. By killing this man, he could throw a scare into the remaining five because they could not be sure who was responsible.

He picked up his speed, even though his breath was growing short. He wasn't used to running. A man got used to riding everywhere he went, even if it was only a hundred yards or so. But he kept going, rifle held across his chest. He had little hope that he could kill the man ahead of him without firing.

He was drawing close now. He could tell from the sounds coming from ahead of him.

And suddenly he was appalled at himself.

Here he was, sheriff of Cruces County, intent on murdering a man in cold blood if it was necessary.

But this was a special situation, requiring special measures. Without warning the outlaw and his horse came into view.

The man saw him at almost the same instant. Hines it was, the one who had tried to rip the clothes off Lily, who had pawed and molested her every chance he got. This was the one she had brought the stack of dishes down upon, the one she had threatened with the pan of hot water until Pew ordered him to desist. This was the one who would rape and kill Lily before he left this place if he was not stopped.

To have the man turn out to be Hines made what Sam had to do easier. Hines dragged his revolver from its holster, his surprise at seeing Sam appear so suddenly evident in his face.

Sam's rifle already had a cartridge in the chamber. He swung it toward Hines, risked the time necessary to raise it to his shoulder, sighted it on the center of Hines's chest and fired.

Hines fired at almost the same time, but coming a fraction of a second later, his bullet missed Sam by at least three feet. Hines was driven back out of his saddle by the heavy rifle slug striking his breastbone squarely. Sam knew he was dead without looking because he knew exactly where his bullet had gone.

Before the outlaw's horse could run away, he

caught him and stripped saddle and bridle from him. The loose horse moved to join the others, now farther downstream. Turning, Sam ran as swiftly as he could, also downstream, staying on the grassy, leaf-strewn floor of the creek bottom so that his trail could not be followed easily.

One, Hines, was dead. But five were still left, and the five still held Jimmy hostage. Furthermore, the shots had surely been heard by the gunrunners up at the house. They might even have been heard by Villa and his men, who must be close by now.

Sam ran until he was exhausted and had to stop and rest. He listened intently for sounds behind him, but he could hear nothing.

Now, he must work his way back to the position he had held earlier, without being heard or seen. But satisfaction was strong in him despite his knowledge that very little had been changed. He had, at least, done something. He had cut the number of outlaws from six to five. He had deprived them of their horses, which might, in the end, prove to be crucial.

Moving as quietly as he could, he headed back, stopping at frequent intervals to listen. They now knew someone was here, someone hostile who would kill them one by one if he could. They'd be looking for him and they'd kill him on sight.

CHAPTER THIRTEEN

Villa was picking his way down the shallow slope when he heard the shots. They seemed to be at least a quarter mile away.

He glanced warily around. His men were spread out behind him, keeping, as he had instructed, an interval of twenty or thirty feet between them so that a burst from the machine guns wouldn't wipe out his whole command.

The three gunrunners manning the machine guns had them pointed his way. The four who had been playing cards on the ground beside one of the wagons were now standing up. Another man, who had gone into the house, now came out, closed the door behind him, and stood on the stoop, peering at Villa and his men, approaching but still nearly a quarter mile away.

Suddenly Villa decided he did not like this situation at all. He halted his horse and turned his head. He bellowed an order, directing one of his officers to take fifteen men, move right into the creek bottom, and advance along it until they had ascertained who had been shooting at whom and why.

The officer swiftly selected his men, calling them by name. Then, leading them, he trotted his horse away at right angles to the creek. Villa sat motionless until they had disappeared.

Now he called another of his men, a private this time but one who spoke English almost as well as he did Spanish. He said, 'Ride down there and tell Dillman to get those men away from the machine guns. Tell him if he does not, the deal is off.'

The young man rode away, recklessly galloping his horse down the slope, pulling him up, plunging, where Dillman stood alone before the house. He said, 'Señor, El General has ordered me to tell you to get your men away from the wagons and the machine guns mounted on their seats. He says to tell you that if you do not do so the deal is off.'

Dillman frowned. He knew he and his men were covered by the group down in the creek bottom, and that they could open fire at any time if what they intended was to take over the guns and sell them to Villa themselves. Still, that didn't seem too likely, particularly in view of the fact that the two shots, which Dillman had heard faintly from within the house and which had brought him out the door, had given their presence away.

He shouted at the men on the wagon seats. 'Get down off the wagons and then all seven of you move away from the wagons for at least thirty feet. But keep the wagons between you and the creek.'

The machine gunners looked a bit uncertain momentarily, but they obeyed, climbed down, and moved away from the wagons along with the other four. Dillman looked at the young Mexican. 'Tell Señor Villa we have done as he has asked. Tell him there are some men in the creek bottom who are not with us but who I think intend to try robbing us of the money as soon as it has been paid.'

The young man galloped his horse back up the rise to where Villa still sat his fidgeting horse. He relayed the message to Villa, translating it as accurately as he could.

Villa scowled. His eyes, usually mild, were narrowed and dangerous. He smelled a trap here and he didn't like riding into it. Dillman's men could get back to the machine guns quickly enough, knowing any gunfire from Villa's galloping men would not be accurate.

God only knew how many men were hiding down there in the creek. He had seen but two but that didn't mean only two were there. It could be a regiment of the U.S. Army, for all he knew, only waiting to open fire until he and his men came into range.

He stared longingly at the wagons, the double teams of mules still hitched to them, the cargo they carried covered over with canvas and lashed down tight. For all he knew, the wagons did not contain rifles at all. They might have empty boxes in them, or lumber, or anything that would look like cases of rifles, particularly with canvas covers over them.

Villa said to the young interpreter, 'Go tell him to come up here and we will talk.'

113

The young man rode away for the second time. Villa and his men stayed where they were. Villa wasn't afraid, no matter how many men were hiding in the bed of the creek. But he did fear those machine guns because he knew what they could do to his command. He didn't understand their presence because no deal had been made for machine guns and he wanted to hear from Dillman himself why they were here.

The young man approached Dillman and spoke to him. Dillman hesitated a few moments but finally walked to the wagon where his horse was tied. The saddle still was on but he had to tighten the cinch before he could mount.

Having done so, he threw an uneasy glance toward the creek bottom, then followed the young man toward the rise where Villa sat his horse.

As he left the ranch yard, he called to his men, 'Don't get too far away from those machine guns. There's men down there in the creek bottom and they're either going to try and take the guns or kill us and take the money after the exchange is made.'

The machine gunners began to edge slowly and surreptitiously closer to their guns. A dozen feet behind the ragged private, Dillman rode up the hill, toward the big, unshaven man with the mustache who was waiting there for him.

Down in the creek bottom, Pew saw the

contingent under the young officer break away from the main body of Villa's troops and head at right angles toward the bushy bottom of the creek.

Now, he thought furiously, he was boxed in on both sides. He had heard the shots downstream, and, since Hines had not returned, was forced to assume that Hines had lost the duel with whomever he had come up against.

The loss of Hines worried him, because Dillman had seven men besides himself and now, because of those shots, was warned that somebody was here, probably intending to try and rob him of the money after he had collected it for the guns.

But even more than the loss of Hines, the presence of an unknown person or persons worried him. He had no way of knowing if there was one man, a handful, or a regiment. The Army might somehow have gotten word that the gun sale was taking place today. Hines might have run into them, pulled his gun, and been shot down for his pains.

Or it might be the customs men. Whoever it was, they would be more interested in driving Villa back into Mexico than in fighting him. The trouble was, if Villa was driven back into Mexico, the money he'd brought to pay for the guns would go with him and all anybody would have would be the six wagonloads of guns and ammunition, which the Army would promptly confiscate.

Al Brunner asked, 'What the hell do we do now?'

Pew thought about that a moment, frowning. There was no place he and his men could hide. Not from that Mexican officer and his men. The only chance any of them had was to open fire on the Mexicans, kill as many as possible, and force them to dismount and fight on foot. Then, and only then, could they have a chance to get away. He said, 'Spread out in a line. Get the best cover you can find. Each of you pick yourself a man but be sure you get the one you pick. Get a second if you can. Then, when they dismount, begin shooting their horses until the rest of them have run away. Let's put them on foot like us.'

'Villa will bring his whole damn command down here.'

Pew shook his head. 'No he won't, because he don't know who's down here or how many of us there are. For all he knows there's a regiment of U.S. Cavalry here.'

The young Mexican officer and his fifteen men were now close enough so that the crashing of brush made by the horses moving through it was plainly audible. Pew's men scattered, each finding the best cover available, a thick bush, the trunk of a willow tree, a large rock, or a depression in the ground. And they waited.

The lieutenant was both young and

inexperienced, because instead of spreading his men as skirmishers, he brought them on in a solid body, himself riding in the lead.

Pew got a careful bead on the center of the lieutenant's chest, knowing that if their commander was dead, the men would become demoralized.

Closer and closer came the Mexicans. They were about forty feet away when the lieutenant saw Pew, saw the bore of Pew's rifle centered squarely on his chest.

There was no more time left than for his eyes to widen with surprise and for his rifle to begin to raise. Then Pew fired.

Struck squarely in the chest, the lieutenant was driven back. He tumbled from his saddle, dead before he hit the ground. Pew fired at the man immediately behind him, and saw this one go down too.

The others now were firing. Seven of the lieutenant's fifteen men were knocked from their saddles. Five horses were brought down, either dead or wounded, before the others turned and stampeded away in fright. The Mexicans still alive had dismounted when the firing began, but so far had not gotten off more than half a dozen ineffectual shots at Pew and his men, who were already retreating in the heavy underbrush.

Then there was utter silence in the creek bottom. The Mexicans, shocked by what had happened to them so swiftly, stayed prone and hidden for awhile, still uncertain as to exactly what they had come up against. Then, satisfied that their attackers had gone, they got up and went to the lieutenant and their fallen comrades.

The lieutenant was dead, and so were three of the others. Four were wounded, one seriously, the other three superficially.

Helping their wounded, but leaving the dead behind, the beaten contingent of Villa's troops began their retreat, back to the gentle slope where Villa sat his horse talking with Dillman through the interpreter.

*   *   *

Villa heard the burst of gunfire and paid little attention to it. He had sent the lieutenant down into the creek bottom to clear out whoever was there and it sounded like he was doing it.

Sam, who had watched the sixteen men separate themselves from Villa's main body of troops, now could only wonder what was happening. He knew Pew and the others must have seen the detachment approaching. Pew would have been faced with few options: trying to hide himself and his men, standing and fighting, or fleeing before Villa's mounted troops. None of his choices was very palatable. Nor was the first choice very satisfactory because while the creek bottom had brushy growth and trees in it, there was no place five

118

men could completely hide themselves.

Sam knew instinctively the course Pew would choose. They'd stand firm and ambush Villa's troops, and then in the confusion would try to make good their escape.

Having done so, he asked himself, what would Pew do then? He would know he couldn't hide forever, nor would he be lucky a second time trying to ambush Villa's men.

Jimmy would be useless as a hostage as far as Villa was concerned. He would also be useless as far as Dillman was concerned.

Listening intently, Sam waited. He heard the sudden crackling of rifle fire from a quarter mile upstream. It was soon over, having come in only two volleys, the first, a shattering one and the second, a more scattered one.

Sam tried to guess what had happened, knowing what he knew about Pew and his men. They would have concealed themselves and laid an ambush for the Mexicans. That first shattering volley had probably brought down the Mexican commander and at least half his men. Pew would also have tried to kill as many horses as possible, hoping to scare the others away.

From the sound of it, he had been as successful as he had hoped to be. Which meant he would be retreating, coming this way as swiftly as he could on foot. He and his men would find the body of Hines and the saddle and bridle of Hines's horse. They wouldn't take the time to try reading tracks on the ground, so they still wouldn't know who was here in the creek bed with them, who had killed Hines, or how many men they were up against.

After they had passed this spot, what would they do then? They'd know that Villa would send more men to avenge the losses he had sustained. Or would he? Wouldn't Villa be more interested in first securing the guns, particularly the machine guns mounted on their seats? Of course he would. He'd ignore what had happened to his small detachment and concentrate on getting possession of the guns.

Sam moved away downstream. He could hear Pew and his four remaining men as they came crashing through the brush. Once he heard Jimmy cry out with pain, probably as he was scratched by a brushy branch.

At least the boy was still alive and relatively unhurt. There was comfort for Sam in that.

CHAPTER FOURTEEN

Villa, sitting his horse on the slope with Dillman, turned his head and looked at the string of three pack horses. Their panniers were loaded with iron-bound boxes which contained the money he had brought to pay for the guns. There had been a discussion between

120

him and his senior officers as to how much real money should be packaged with the 'Villa money' to make the packages look real. How deeply, they had tried to decide, would the gunrunners riffle through the money packages?

Finally it had been decided that a half-dozen American bills were to be placed on the outside of each of the packages on the top layer. The lower rows would be faced with a single U.S. note.

Even if Dillman saw the peso notes sandwiched in between there was a good chance that, unless he actually opened one of the packages, he would assume that the peso notes were good ones, guaranteed by the Mexican Government and not by Villa alone.

The men who had gone into the creek bottom came straggling up the slope, carrying one of their wounded, helping the others who did not appear to be as seriously hurt. Villa saw that, of the sixteen men who had gone into the creek bottom, only twelve were coming back and that four of these twelve were wounded.

Fury touched him and his eyes blazed. For a moment, he considered taking his entire command down there into that creek bottom and sweeping it clean of whoever was hiding there.

Then, imperceptibly, he shook his head. The machine guns first, and the wagonloads of guns. Then there would be time for ridding himself of everyone who had seen the exchange take place and that included the men in the creek bottom who had killed his lieutenant and three of his men. He ordered, as the men approached with their wounded, 'Take them to the house and have the woman take care of their wounds.' To one of the men he said, 'You. What happened?'

'We ran into an ambush, General.'

'I can see that, fool! How many men ambushed you?'

'We could not tell for sure, General, but there must have been twenty or thirty at least.'

Villa knew from experience that any estimate he was likely to get in a situation like this would be larger than the actual count. But he let the man go, having more important things on his mind right now than disciplining a soldier who, after all, had only done what he was told.

Villa's rifle was carried across his knees, fully loaded, a fine Winchester carbine with a lever-operated action that could be fired rapidly. Suddenly he jacked a cartridge into the chamber and swung the muzzle to cover Dillman. Through the young interpreter he said, 'We will ride down to the ranch house, Señor Dillman. We will take possession of the guns, and we will position the wagons on which the machine guns are mounted so that we can fire them in any direction without having to worry about gunfire from the rear.'

Dillman looked into the bore of Villa's

carbine. He knew how unpredictable Villa was, and he knew that any sudden distraction, even a single shot from the bed of the creek, would probably cause the Mexican to pull the trigger and kill him instantly.

His face may have turned a little paler but otherwise he managed not to show any fear. He shrugged lightly and nodded. 'That's all right with me. They're your guns just as soon as we get paid.'

'What about the machine guns? I did not bring money to pay for them.'

'We'll dismantle two of them and put them in the wagons. You can have them with our compliments. The third, we'll mount on one of the buildings to make sure you try no treachery on us, Señor General.'

For an instant Villa's eyes blazed and his face turned hard. Then, unexpectedly, he laughed. 'All right, let's get on down there.' He waved an arm to beckon his men after him and, with Dillman and the interpreter, rode down the shallow slope. All the men started to follow him but, in Spanish, he bellowed an order for a score of them to remain behind as reserves.

They reached the bottom of the hill. Through the young interpreter, Villa told Dillman, 'Tell your men to drive the wagons on which the guns are mounted up against the house, two on the sides facing the creek, one on the side facing the road.'

In Spanish, Villa ordered three of his own

men to mount the wagon seats along with the gringo teamsters to make sure they did not try to use the guns.

Dillman grumbled, 'You sure as hell don't trust me much, do you?'

'I trust no one, señor.'

'I never tried to double-cross you before.'

'But there were never this many guns involved.'

Dillman shrugged. The wounded were carried into the house. Lily showed where to put them. Then she came to the door and looked at Dillman. Villa bowed gallantly, taking off his hat. He smiled engagingly at her. She only half returned his smile and nodded absently to him. Worriedly she said, 'I heard shooting down in the creek. What do you think . . . ?'

Dillman said, 'I think that bunch under Pew laid an ambush for the soldiers Villa sent down there after them. They killed four and wounded four. Then they beat a retreat.'

'Did any of the Mexicans see my little boy?'

Dillman asked the question of Villa, through the interpreter. The interpreter yelled at one of the men who had been present during the skirmish and put the question to him. The man shook his head.

Lily wasn't satisfied. Fearfully now, she asked Dillman, 'Ask him if they followed those men at all. Ask him if he's sure they didn't leave my little boy behind.'

The question was asked and answered in Spanish. Then the interpreter said, 'No, señora, they did not see a boy. They followed for only a hundred yards and then gave up. But they did not see a boy. Dead or alive.'

Dead. That was what Lily feared—that Pew and his men would kill Jimmy the first time they got into a fight simply because he was in the way.

The three wagons rolled up close to the house, positioning themselves, one in the front and the others on each side of the building, so that the machine guns would be able to cover almost every possible approach. The other wagons remained where they were. Villa asked of Dillman, 'How long since the mules have been watered and fed?'

'Yesterday afternoon. We have been trying to rest by day and travel by night.'

Villa nodded, satisfied that the mules were in sufficiently good shape to travel the twenty miles between here and the border of Mexico.

Having positioned the wagons with the machine guns, and having satisfied himself that the teams could make the trip into Mexico, Villa now ordered, through the interpreter, that all the gringos go into the ranch house.

Dillman protested and his protests were duly relayed to Villa, who shook his head inflexibly and pointed to the building.

Dillman called his men and they all trooped into the house. Dillman thought that Villa was

125

now in complete control of the situation. He had the rifles and all three machine guns. He also still had the money that was to have been paid for them. Dillman began to wonder if Villa had any money at all, if the boxes loaded into the pack horses panniers weren't empty.

Villa and the interpreter started to leave, Villa apparently reluctant because of his admiration for Lily. Dillman was relieved that Villa hadn't taken their guns away from them. He would take Villa prisoner right here and now and hold him until the money had been paid.

He discarded the idea at once. Threatening Villa would be the most foolish thing he could do. Besides, he thought, maybe it would be a good idea if Villa and his men did remain in control outside. Villa might send another detachment to clear Pew and his men out of the creek bottom.

Still puzzling were the shots he had heard before Villa sent that patrol down to investigate. Was it possible that Pew had had a fight with one of his own men? Anything was possible, he thought. But he knew of Pew's presence and intentions and he figured he and his seven men could handle them.

All that remained, then, was to get the money and for Villa to leave. Then he could worry about Pew.

Villa and his interpreter went out. Dillman glanced at Lily and saw her worried expression, the tears shining in her eyes. He wished briefly that there was something he could do about her little boy but there was not. Pew wouldn't accept a partial ransom for him even if Dillman had been willing to pay it. But maybe Pew wouldn't kill him. Maybe he was just making threats.

Dillman didn't really believe that, though. When this was over with, the boy would be dead. And if Pew should happen to win out he would also kill the boy's mother and the Mexican cowhand. He wouldn't want anybody left who could identify him. He would want the slaughter to look like Villa's work.

So he and his men would be protecting Lily and her Mexican cowboy when they fought with Pew. Damn it, she couldn't expect more from him than that.

Sam Chance's horse was at least a mile up the creek from where he now was, but the horse was tied securely and it was doubtful if anyone, either Pew's men or Villa's, would stumble onto him. He was safe for now, and available to Sam when he needed him.

When he had seen the small detachment of Villa's men head for the creek bottom and disappear, he had dared to hope, briefly, that Pew would drop Jimmy as excess baggage when he fled from the Mexicans.

But it hadn't worked that way. Apparently Pew and those with him had laid an ambush for the Mexicans. The fight had been short and furious and now Sam saw the Mexicans who had survived helping their wounded comrades back up the gentle slope. Villa's losses were four men dead, he thought, and four wounded. Villa wouldn't forget that. He'd go back, with a large force, and next time he'd find Pew's men, engage and kill them all.

When that happened, Jimmy would be one of the first casualties. To Pew, in a stiff fight with superior numbers, Jimmy would simply be a nuisance, not worth the loss of the man required to keep an eye on him. He'd probably just knock Jimmy in the head with his gun barrel and leave him where he fell.

Sam thought of Lily. He could imagine the anguish she was going through. She wouldn't know but what Pew had already killed Jimmy. Pew's presence was now known both to Dillman and his gunrunners and to Villa and his men, so Jimmy no longer had any hostage value to Pew. There was no reason for Pew to continue to let him live.

Sam began to pick his way toward the place from which the recent sounds of battle had come. He'd never be able to face Lily when this was over if he didn't do his best to rescue her son.

He moved cautiously, testing each footstep before he let his weight fall onto the foot. Pew's men wouldn't be traveling as carefully as he was, but neither would they be crashing through the underbrush, careless of the noise they made.

Sam had his rifle in his hands. His knuckles were white, so tightly was he holding it. He was scared for Jimmy, more scared than he had ever been in his life before. He was also scared that if anything happened to Jimmy, while he was here within a few hundred yards, that Lily wouldn't ever want to see him again.

He thought, 'Damn! Damn! Why did they have to pick this place for their lousy gun exchange?'

CHAPTER FIFTEEN

Villa was not gone from the adobe house for very long. Dillman, watching from the window, saw him ride up the slope to where he had left his reserves. He talked to their commander several moments, gesturing both toward the house and the creek bottom as he did. Then he rode back down the hill.

Lily MacDonald, assisted by her Mexican cowhand, was caring for the wounds sustained by Villa's men. They were mostly leg and arm wounds, and apparently no bones or arteries had been hit. The fourth man was something else. He had caught a bullet in the abdomen. When Lily had finished bandaging him, she came out into the kitchen. The ambulatory wounded had already left. In reply to

Dillman's questioning glance she said, 'There is nothing I can do for him. He is bleeding inside and the bullet is still there. I don't know enough to try to get it out, or to try and repair the damage that it did.'

'Villa knows you're not a doctor. He won't expect miracles.'

'I suppose not. But I wish there was something I could do for that poor man. He's in terrible pain. You can see it in his face and his eyes but he does not cry out.'

Villa, having stationed all his men outside, some near or behind the wagons, some in various outbuildings, now returned to the house accompanied by his interpreter. Through him he said to Dillman, 'I want to see the guns.'

'And I want to see the money.'

Villa nodded. 'All right, señor. The guns first.'

Dillman followed him out the door. He unlashed the canvas cover on one of the wagons that still stood out in the yard. He pulled it back. From the wagon toolbox he got a bar and pried the cover off one of the cases.

Inside were the rifles, still covered with the grease designed to keep them from rusting until they were issued and put to use. Villa said, 'Another box.' He pointed. 'This one.'

Dillman opened the box. It also contained rifles. Villa pointed to one of the wagons beside the house. 'Let us look in that one, señor.'

Dillman followed him to the wagon and took the lashings off. Again he pried open a couple of boxes which Villa, this time, selected from among those on the bottom layer. Apparently satisfied that there were guns in all the boxes in all the wagons, Villa beckoned one of his men who was near the string of pack animals. Grinning, he looked at Dillman and spoke in Spanish to the interpreter. The man said, 'The general asks if you want to select a box.'

Dillman picked a box and the soldier pulled it from the pannier. Villa himself knelt and opened it. It was filled with bundles of money, each approximately an inch thick.

Villa tossed one to Dillman, who saw the United States yellowbacks on the outside and did not bother to riffle through the bundle. He said, 'Another box,' apparently more worried that not all the boxes contained money than he was that not all the bundles were U.S. yellowbacks clear through.

Villa quickly turned his face away. He ordered the soldier to get a box from another pack. The soldier obeyed and again Villa knelt and opened the box. This time, Dillman didn't even bother to take a bundle of money out.

He asked that a third box be opened and it was. This time, he knelt and dug through the money all the way to the bottom, once more failing to look beyond the bills on the outside of the packages.

Villa looked at Dillman. He spoke to the young interpreter, who said, 'El General wants to know if you are satisfied, señor.'

Dillman nodded. He was satisfied and he knew Villa was satisfied.

Now Villa pointed to the house, indicating that Dillman was to return to it. Frowning slightly with concern, Dillman obeyed. He was hardly in a position not to obey.

Villa began shouting orders in Spanish to his men. They went to their horses, mounted, and formed a ragged column. Villa sent a man riding up the slope to relay his orders to the reserves. They moved on down the slope and positioned themselves just outside of rifle range, but in a spot from which they could cover the front door of the house.

Dillman glanced around at his men. 'I don't know why, but I've got a feeling in my guts that something's wrong.'

Jake Gwin asked, 'The money was all right, wasn't it? You looked in three boxes. Did you try counting any of it?'

Dillman shook his head. 'It was in bank wrappers, a thousand dollars to the package. It looked all right.'

'Then what could be wrong? Villa's taking his men down into the creek bottom now. He'll track Pew and what's left of his bunch and kill them like a nest of mice.'

Phil Hibbert said, 'That bunch came here to rob and kill us after Villa left. At least we won't have to worry about them any more.'

Dillman nodded. He had to agree. He didn't see what there could be in this situation to make him feel so uneasy. But the uneasiness couldn't be rationalized away. It remained.

Lily, who had gone into the bedroom, now came out. 'The man that was shot in the abdomen just died.'

Nobody said anything. With her voice tight with fear, Lily said, 'When Villa attacks them they'll kill my boy. The only value he had to them was to keep me or Pedro from giving their presence away. Now that it's known, they have no further use for him.'

Dillman couldn't look at her. The silence became awkward and finally he said, 'I'm sorry, ma'am. If there was anything I could do, I would.'

She nodded numbly, walked across to the window, and stared outside. Tears filled her eyes and ran across her cheeks. Sam was Jimmy's only chance, she thought, and what could Sam do against Pew and those with him? They were absolutely vicious and he was outnumbered at least six to one. He might kill one or two of them before they got him but that wouldn't save Jimmy's life.

Villa took his detachment, about thirty-five men in all, down the cutbank into the creek bed immediately below the house. He sent his Tarahumara Indian scout ahead to find the outlaws' tracks. After a few moments the man

133

beckoned and pointed to the ground. 'Five men, señor, on foot. They are hurrying and they are going that way.' The Indian pointed downstream.

Villa said, 'Follow them.'

The Indian remained on foot, leading his horse. He moved along at a fast walk, sometimes nearly a trot. Villa and his men kept a distance behind him of forty or fifty feet.

Sam, on the other side of the nearly dry stream and on foot himself, saw the Indian find the trail, saw him turn to follow it, and saw Villa and his men follow the Indian.

He knew that if Villa's soldiers reached Pew and the remaining four before he did, Jimmy was as good as dead. He also knew that even if he beat Villa to Pew, his chance of saving Jimmy's life was negligible.

Nevertheless, he turned and, staying out of sight in the brush and trees, he ran downstream, paralleling the course being taken by the Villistas and their Tarahumara tracker.

He didn't worry about making noise, knowing the Villistas were making so much themselves that there was no chance of their hearing him. After traveling about half a mile, the Tarahumara apparently found Hines and the saddle and bridle from Hines's horse. Villa and the guide discussed this in Spanish, which Sam could not understand, so rapidly did they speak. Then, Villa put two flankers out on either side of the Indian and a little bit ahead of him. Sam thought this was because Villa didn't want to lose the services of the Tarahumara tracker if it could be helped.

Sam was able to stay about a couple of hundred yards ahead of the tracker and the flankers but he was seldom able to see them.

He therefore risked abandoning the brush and instead took to the open, sandy bed of the meandering stream. He was running hard now, and out of breath because he wasn't used to it.

Behind him, he heard a shout. Immediately rifle fire crackled.

Sam stopped in his tracks. An expression of dismay crossed his face. Jimmy was almost certainly dead by now. Killing him was one of the first things Pew would have done when Villa caught up with him and attacked.

There was nothing on earth that he could do. Intervening in the gun battle going on less than four hundred yards from him would only ensure his death. He'd have to wait, and when the battle stopped, find Jimmy's body and take it back to where he had left his horse.

Feeling utterly miserable, feeling he had let Lily down the first time she had really needed him, he waited. The firing slackened and finally stopped. Moving silently, Sam got to a spot that was within earshot of Villa's men. Edging even closer, he could see them, some still mounted, some now off their horses examining the bodies of those that they had killed.

There were only three, and Jimmy's was not one of them. Villa gave orders in Spanish to the Indian tracker and to about half a dozen men. Tracker and horsemen moved away, still following the trail. Villa and the rest of his men turned and retraced their course up the creek bed and toward the adobe ranch house they had left only a few minutes before.

Elated, Sam waited until both groups had disappeared from sight. Then he hurried to the spot where three dead bodies lay. Pew and Quigley were the ones who had escaped. And, he thought, they must still have Jimmy because his body was not here.

Immediately, Sam took the trail left by the Indian tracker and the half dozen mounted Villistas who were following him. He knew that he still didn't dare to hope. Jimmy might not be dead yet, but his chances of surviving were no better than they had been a little while ago.

Trotting soundlessly, Sam Chance followed the plain trail left by the seven Villista horses in the brush, grass, and leaves of the creek bottom.

CHAPTER SIXTEEN

Arch Dillman's worry did not decrease, despite the fact that Villa had taken a sizable number of men into the creek bottom to flush out and get rid of the outlaws. It continued even though he knew that once Pew and his men were eliminated, the rifle sale could go forward in an orderly manner just the way all his previous arms deals with Villa had gone.

He and his men, Lily MacDonald, and her cowhand Pedro Ramirez were, for the moment, alone in the house. Outside, the reserves still waited on the slope for Villa's orders, probably three or four hundred yards away. Three men still manned the machine guns mounted on the wagon seats. A few others, numbering maybe a dozen, stood beside the wagons, looking toward the creek bed into which Villa and his men had disappeared.

Dillman said, 'I've been feeling funny all morning. Now I think that I know why.'

Saul Ernst, the most nervous of them all, asked, 'Why?'

'That money. I never did riffle through any of those packages to see if the notes were the same all the way through. And about a month ago I heard that Villa was printing his own money in Chihuahua guaranteed by nothing more than his own signature.'

Ernst said, 'Oh my God! You think he's packaged a lot of that money with a few U.S. notes on the outside of each package?'

'It's possible.'

Ernst said accusingly, 'You should have

137

looked through each package. You...'

Dillman agreed, 'Yes. I suppose I should. But don't lay it all on me. You could have checked that money too.'

'So what do we do?'

'Find out, first of all, whether the money's good or not.'

'And how do you propose to do that? Every one of those wooden chests is out in the panniers on those pack horses.'

'We've got to get one of the chests.'

'How? For God's sake, man, there's twenty or more reserves up on the slope. And there must be a dozen men hanging around the house.'

Dillman said, 'Villa has gone down into the creek bottom after Pew and his men. They'll catch them in a little bit, and when they do, I figure every one of the Mexican soldiers Villa left behind will be looking toward where all the sound of gunfire is coming from.'

Ernst said, 'Maybe. But if one of them isn't, you're dead.'

'If that money's phony, all of us are dead anyhow.'

Jake Gwin, one of Dillman's steadiest men, said, 'When the shooting starts, all of us could run outside. There's no reason we can't act as curious as those Mexicans. We'll walk as far toward the creek as we can. I figure when we get thirty or forty yards from the house, those Mexicans will get edgy and come after us.

Every damn one of them is going to be looking at us and that might give you time enough to run out and get one of those money chests.'

Dillman looked around at the other men. 'What about it? Does that sound like a good idea to the rest of you?'

'It's risky,' Frank Helder said, 'but we've got to know about the money while there's still time to plan how we're going to come out of this alive.'

'All right then. It's settled.'

'What about the machine gunner in front of the house? What if he won't leave his gun?'

'Then it won't work. I figure, though, that he'll yell at all of you to stop when you go running out of here. He won't fire without Villa's command. When you don't stop running, he's likely to panic and get down off the wagon and come after you.'

All the men agreed, except Ernst, whose face was pale, whose hands were trembling. Dillman stared at him without sympathy. He said, 'You bought a bunch of stolen guns and figured to double your money on them. You knew it would be dangerous, so don't try to weasel out of what's got to be done now.'

Ernst's face flushed. He grumbled, 'I'll do what the rest of you do.'

'All right then. I'll open the door a crack so we can hear the first shots. As soon as Villa and that bunch start raising hell down there, all of you go running out. Circle the house and go about halfway between the creek bed and the house. Act like you're trying to see something. As soon as the Mexicans take after you, I'll get one of those money chests. They aren't very big and there's a lot of them, so one shouldn't be missed. At least not right away.'

All the men crowded close to the door. Dillman stood back. Lily watched him with eyes that held a hopeless look. She believed, he thought, that when Villa's forces found and engaged Pew and his friends, Jimmy would be the first casualty. Behind her Pedro said softly, 'Pray, señora. It is all you can do now.'

She nodded, closed her eyes. Her lips moved soundlessly.

Suddenly, distantly, a volley of rapid fire broke out. Instantly all of Dillman's men, except himself, rushed out the door. The Mexican on the seat of the wagon positioned before the house yelled at them in Spanish, but they paid no attention and ran on. There was a lot more shouting in Spanish. The Mexican got down from the wagon and ran after the men, yelling at his companions in Spanish, which none of those in the house, except for Pedro, understood. Dillman was already out the door, running toward the pack horses, as Pedro said, 'They are shouting at the gringos to come back or they will shoot.'

Dillman reached the pack horses. The same box he had examined before was on top, so he seized it and raced back toward the house. He burst into the door, without a shot having been fired at him. Lily, standing at the window and watching the reserves up on the slope, had not seen any of them glance this way and knew none of them had seen Dillman seize the box.

The shooting in the creek bottom had stopped. Now both the Mexicans and Dillman's men came straggling back. The Mexicans stayed outside. Dillman's men came in. Ernst was shaking violently and looked as if he was going to be sick. He said in a shaky voice, 'I thought we were goners. I thought they were going to shoot.'

Jake Gwin asked, 'Get the box?'

Dillman nodded. 'It's in the bedroom. Let's get in there and take a look at it.'

All of them started to crowd into the bedroom but Dillman said, 'Five of you stay out here. Gwin and I will look at the money. We'll know soon enough.'

Dillman went into the bedroom, followed closely by Jake Gwin. He opened the lid and snatched up one of the money packages. He riffled through it, his stomach suddenly feeling empty as he did. The notes on the outside of the bundle were U.S. yellowbacks. The rest were brand new, Villista notes adorned with Francisco Villa's signature.

He looked at two more packages and both were the same. He closed the box and shoved it under the bed. He went out into the kitchen, noticing that the Mexican gunner was back at

141

his post beside the machine gun on the wagon seat.

He was sick with disappointment and his face was livid with rage. He said, 'That dirty double-crossing Mexican sonofabitch! I doubt if there's a thousand dollars in real money in all those boxes he's got. The rest is Villista money and the goddam ink isn't dry on it yet.'

The faces of the other men reflected varying emotions, but there was fury in all of them. Only Pedro Ramirez's face reflected his dismay. He said, 'Señor, you know what this means?'

'What?'

'That he cannot leave anyone here alive. He has twenty miles to go with those wagons before he reaches Mexico. It is a long day's journey at the very least. If he leaves you behind, knowing how you have been cheated, he knows you will go to the U.S. Army and have him intercepted before he reaches Mexico. He cannot afford to take that chance.'

Villa and his men rode back into the yard, raising a huge cloud of dust. Lily glanced quickly at every man, but none of them was carrying the slight body of her five-year-old son. A slow sigh of relief escaped her because she believed that if Villa had found her son dead he would have brought the body back. He'd had his eye on her and would do this in the hope of pleasing her.

Which meant, she thought with a hope that

was somehow forlorn, that Jimmy might still be alive.

Suddenly she heard two more shots. She could stand the uncertainty no more. Beckoning Pedro to act as interpreter, she rushed from the house and ran to where Villa was. 'Ask him if he saw Jimmy.'

Pedro asked, in Spanish.

Villa looked at Lily, the same admiration for her still in his eyes. He spoke rapidly in Spanish and Pedro translated for her. 'He says they pursued five men, having found one already dead. They caught and killed three of them, but the other two escaped, one of them no doubt is carrying your son. He says he has sent his Tarahumara Indian tracker and several men after them and that they ought to catch and kill them soon. He says he has given orders to his men to save your son's life if it is possible.'

Lily thought of the shots she had just heard fired, distantly and far downstream. Could these have been the shots that killed the remaining two outlaws? Was Jimmy still alive? Almost as if she was in a daze, she turned and went back into the house. Her heart felt numb, her chest tight with fear. How could she stand to wait? And yet she believed, as did Dillman and his men, that Villa was going to slaughter everyone here before he took the six wagonloads of guns and ammunition and rode away.

Still, something might yet happen to change

everything. Last night things had seemed hopeless, with Pew and his dirty gang of cutthroats here and in control. Things seemed no less hopeless now. But the situation had changed last night and it might well change again. Sam Chance was somewhere out there...

One man against seventy or more. She made herself remember his face, so calm, so very strong, so self-assured. He'd have to perform a miracle to save their lives. But if anyone on earth could perform that miracle, it would be Sam. How could she have put him off, she wondered now to herself. Both of them might die without knowing the joy of being together.

Never again would she let anything stop her when her heart told her it was right. But that pledge to herself depended on surviving the rest of today and tonight. She looked at Pedro, her eyes brimming with tears. Reverting to his native tongue, which she only partially understood, he said, 'Señora, God will find a way. Have faith in Him.'

Numbly she nodded, not knowing how much of her faith was in God and how much was in Sam Chance.

CHAPTER SEVENTEEN

Dillman went to the window and stood beside Lily MacDonald. He stared out at Villa, sitting his horse like he was part of it, commanding and arrogant.

Dillman knew he had been a fool for engineering such a big deal with Villa. In the past, his gun deals with Villa had never been big enough to make Villa see a need to cheat.

This one, though, was. A hundred thousand dollars was a lot of money to a man who had stolen beef, butchered it, and sold it by the kilo out of his butcher shop. It was a lot of money to a man whose ambition was to march south until Mexico City was in his hands. Dillman knew he should have realized that from the beginning. His failure to realize it was going to cost him his life.

He could hear the men behind him discussing alternatives in lowered tones. Beside him, Lily MacDonald stood, tears running silently down her cheeks. He wondered if the tears were solely for her five-year-old son or whether she, too, knew she was going to die.

He tried to think how they might get out of this alive. The machine guns were the only answer, their only chance. If somehow three of them could get control of the three machine guns, they might be able to shoot down enough of Villa's men to force the rest to run away.

A slim chance, any way you looked at it, he thought wryly. First they had to overpower the men who now manned the guns. And while they were trying to do so, every one of Villa's men would be shooting at them.

But if, by some miracle, they did gain control of the machine guns without first being killed, then they still had to kill every one of Villa's courageous and heavily armed followers. Dillman suspected that few, if any, of Villa's men would run. He also knew that the chance of three men, even with machine guns, killing about seventy others without being killed themselves, was exceedingly slim indeed. But there seemed to be no other alternative.

At least, he thought, they had, so far, not been disarmed. They weren't completely helpless yet.

* * *

Sam Chance, his breath growing short, was having difficulty keeping pace with the tireless Tarahumara scout, and with the Villistas, following him on horseback. He could hear them, drawing away from him now, the sounds of their passage through the brushy creek bottom fading as they did.

He didn't know why he looked behind, but he did. Perhaps he heard the crack of a branch, the dislodging of a rock. But suddenly there they were, great, powerful, bearded Pew, carrying a limp and unconscious Jimmy effortlessly under one arm. And the slighter Quigley, running a little ahead of Pew.

They burst out of the brush that lined the sandy creek bed just as Sam halted and turned his head.

A hundred feet away they were, and they saw Sam the instant he saw them. Both men swung their guns toward him.

Sam's rifle was in his hands. There was a cartridge in the chamber and the hammer was on half cock to prevent accidental discharge. Immediately he thumbed it all the way back, raising the gun, aware that Jimmy might easily be hit when he shot at Pew.

But he had no other choice. The cover of the brushy creek bank was thirty feet away from him. He had been seen and in another instant they would riddle him.

The rifle came up. He could risk a snap shot at Quigley, his racing thoughts told him, but not at Pew. For Pew he had to have accuracy.

Quigley fired at the same instant Sam Chance did. The bullet seared Sam's leg, but he was sure of his own shot because his sights had been centered squarely on Quigley's chest. He dived aside, falling, before the sounds of the two shots had died away. Pew's first bullet missed him by a foot or so, and then he was on the dry, soft sand, trying to get into position for an unhurried, steady shot from a prone position on the ground.

Pew, seeing his first shot miss, believing that Quigley's shot had also missed, now yanked Jimmy's limp, small body around in front of him, using it as a shield. He raised his revolver for another shot at Sam.

Sam lay prone, his belly to the sand. His elbows were in place, his rifle against his shoulder, Ezra Pew in his sights.

He could shoot at Pew's legs with a minimum amount of danger to Jimmy, but that wouldn't stop Pew from shooting and killing him. He didn't dare shoot at Pew's chest or abdomen for fear of hitting the boy. That left Pew's head, at least a foot above Jimmy's head and a reasonably safe target if not a very large one at which to shoot.

Pew fired and the bullet kicked up a geyser of sand no more than six inches to Sam's right. Then Sam's sights came into line.

No time now for his fleeting thoughts to consider what would happen if he missed Pew and killed the boy. He squeezed the trigger perhaps more carefully than ever before in his life, knowing as he did that every second's delay gave Pew another chance to shoot.

The rifle bellowed and belched smoke out in front of him. For just the fraction of a second, Sam Chance couldn't see whether he had hit Pew or not. Then, as the powder smoke cleared, he saw Pew being driven back by the force of the heavy bullet that had struck the solid bone of his skull.

Sam was up and running before Pew hit the ground, jacking in another cartridge as he ran, fully cocking the hammer in case either Pew or Quigley had life left in them.

But neither did. Pew lay on his back, his open but empty eyes staring at the sky. Jimmy, still unconscious, lay partly on his chest and partly off. Quigley was dead, a spreading spot of blood in the exact center of his chest.

Sam understood what the pair had done. Hearing the pursuit of the Tarahumara and Villa's men, they had circled, hoping that back closer to the house they would be able to find a couple of their horses, thus improving their chance to get away. They just hadn't known Sam was where he was.

Gently, Sam picked Jimmy up. He didn't dare wait because if he did the Tarahumara and the Villistas would catch up with him and, not knowing who he was, would kill him instantly. But he took time to look Jimmy over hastily for wounds. He found none but he did find a sizable, bluish lump on the right side of Jimmy's forehead. Something had struck the boy, knocking him out. It might have been deliberate or it might have been an accident.

The boy's breathing was regular, though his face was very pale. Sam hesitated just an instant, while he tried to decide what he should do. He could make it to his horse, mount and ride away, thus saving Jimmy's life and his own. Or he could leave Jimmy someplace where he was not likely to be found and continue trying to find a way of rescuing Lily and Pedro from the house.

The first alternative was intolerable. He couldn't save Jimmy and himself, leaving Lily to die. Nor could he leave Jimmy out here in the brush without knowing how badly the boy was hurt.

The only remaining alternative was the one he decided upon. He must take Jimmy to the house so that Lily could take care of him. That would mean surrendering himself to Villa and it might in the end cost him his life. But he was sheriff. And even Villa might have some respect for the law.

He headed along the sandy creek bed at a trot, hearing already the sounds of the Indian scout and the mounted Villistas growing louder as they drew closer to him. He held Jimmy against his chest, letting Jimmy's head rest limply on his shoulder. In his right hand he carried his rifle, a cartridge in the chamber and the hammer on half cock.

It was now late afternoon. Sam hadn't paid much attention to the passage of time because there had been so many other things on his mind. But now he did.

Villa would probably want to take the wagons to Mexico in the dark if that was possible. There would be less chance of his being seen. That didn't leave much time, since

Villa would probably depart no later than dusk.

Abreast of the house, Sam left the sandy creek bed and headed through the brushy creek bottom toward the house. He came out just below the icehouse, climbed the bank, and walked slowly toward the house.

He was only halfway there when a dozen fierce-looking Villistas surrounded him, seized his rifle, and dug their own gun muzzles into his back.

Anger stirred him but he forced it down. He went straight to the house, ignored Villa, opened the door, and went in.

Lily, who had been watching from the window and had seen him come, met him at the door. Weeping openly, she took Jimmy's limp body from his arms and laid her ear against his chest. A moment passed before she cried, 'He's alive! Oh thank God, he's alive!' She looked up at Sam's face, her eyes brimming, giving him in that one tearful glance all the heartfelt thanks he could have hoped to get. Then she turned and hurried to the bedroom with the boy, where she laid him on the bed.

Sam looked at the gunrunners, one by one. One of them asked, 'Who the hell are you?'

'Sam Chance. I'm the sheriff of this county.'

'How'd you get that kid away from those two?'

'Killed them.'

'Even while they were holding the kid?'

151

'Only one of them was. I'll admit it was a bigger chance than I cared to take. But there wasn't any other way.'

'Then that's the last of the six who were planning to rob us after the gun sale had been made?'

'That's the last of them.'

Dillman stared at him skeptically. 'What are you going to do? Order Villa back to Mexico? Arrest us for running guns?'

Sam grinned faintly. 'That's what I'm supposed to do. But Villa wouldn't go and I wouldn't have much luck trying to arrest the eight of you.'

Dillman said, 'The money's phony. We managed to get a chest of it and he's packaged a bunch of his own fresh-printed money with a few U.S. yellowbacks on the outside. There probably isn't more than a thousand dollars of good money in the whole damn lot.'

Sam had suspected this might be the case. He said, 'You know, then, what he's going to do?'

'Sure. Take the guns and the money and leave every one of us dead. It's the only way he can be sure we won't send the Army after him.'

Sam, who still had his revolver, said, 'Don't let them get your guns away from you if you can help it. Once they do, you haven't got any chance at all.' He pushed his way through the men and went into the bedroom where Lily sat on the bed beside the unconscious form of her son. Sam sat down beside her and put an arm around her waist. 'Do you think he's going to be all right?'

Briefly she laid her cheek against his own. 'I wish we had a doctor here. I don't know what to do.'

'Have you looked him over for other wounds? I gave him a quick once-over when I found him, but I might have missed something.'

She proceeded to undress Jimmy sufficiently to make sure he had sustained no other wounds. 'How did you find him, Sam? How did you get him away from that awful Pew?'

'I'm not sure I want to say.'

'What do you mean by that?'

'I had to hit Pew in the head, and there wasn't much leeway if I missed. Jimmy's head wasn't a foot away.'

'Oh my God!'

'But I was prone on the ground. And I had a steady shot.'

'What about the other one?'

'I didn't have to be so careful with him. I got him first.'

She noticed a wet spot of blood as big as Sam's hand on his pants just above the knee. 'You're hurt.'

'Skinned me.'

'Let me look at it. Jimmy's all right for now. There's nothing I can do for him.'

She took Sam's pocketknife from him and slit his pants from the bottom to above the knee. The bullet gouge was deep, maybe half an inch, and about six inches long. It had bled heavily, but most of the blood had run down Sam's leg rather than soaking through his pants.

Lily got clean flour sacks, ripped them into strips for bandages. She put a thick compress on the wound, then bandaged it with the strips. She ripped down lengthwise the end of the last bandage for eight or ten inches and then, using the two strips, tied the bandage in place. She looked up at him. 'I love you, Sam.'

He kissed her on the mouth, understanding why she was saying this to him right now. She knew that Villa didn't dare leave anyone behind alive. And she didn't see how nine men, even though they still were armed, could prevail against about seventy of Villa's men, who had three machine guns besides their other arms.

Trying to show more confidence than he felt, Sam said, 'As soon as this is over with, we'll go to town, and get the preacher to marry us. We've waited long enough.'

She nodded, without directly meeting his eyes. She didn't believe they'd ever leave this place alive and neither did Sam. But until they were safe there was no sense in telling Sam about her past.

CHAPTER EIGHTEEN

Sam Chance got up from beside Lily on the bed and went out into the kitchen. He said, 'Have you thought about accepting Villa's money for the guns?'

'What good is it? It isn't backed by anything but his signature. And the minute one of the other generals defeats him, it's about as good as that much wallpaper.'

'Maybe nobody's going to defeat him. He's ignorant and crude, but he's a soldier, make no mistake about that. I look for his army to be the biggest in Mexico. I look for him to march on Mexico City and take every town and city along the way. Maybe this Villista money isn't as bad as you think it is.'

'We'd have to go to Mexico to spend it. And each of us will have at least 20,000 pesos to spend.'

Sam grinned. 'Think what a hell of a time you could have. Tequila. Señoritas. Anything you wanted you could buy.'

He was hoping that, if the gunrunners would accept the Villa money, perhaps Villa wouldn't feel it was necessary to murder them. Certainly, if they intended to use the Villa money in Mexico, they would know how worthless it would be if Villa himself was imprisoned in the United States.

'The sonofabitch cheated us.'

Sam shrugged. 'What would you rather be, cheated or dead?'

Dillman said, 'You've got a point. but how are we going to make him believe that we'll take the money and spend it in Mexico?'

That was something Sam didn't know. What he did know was that Villa couldn't take the chance that his wagon convoy would be intercepted before it got to Mexico. There were five thousand repeating rifles in those wagons and he needed them desperately.

Dillman thought about it several moments and finally he said, 'All right. We'll try. It looks like the only chance we've got.' He went into the bedroom and got the money chest out from under the bed. He opened it, took out a couple of bundles, and broke the strips of paper with which they were bound. He spread out the money, Villista currency and yellowbacks, the way a card player might spread a deck of cards. Then he went to the door, beckoning Pedro to act as interpreter. 'Tell him it's time we made the exchange. Tell him I figure he's going to want to leave at dusk.'

Pedro relayed the message to Villa, sitting his horse near the center of the yard.

The Mexican revolutionary ordered some of his men to carry in the money chests. They did, looking surprised and a bit puzzled when they saw the already open chest on the floor with the money spread out on top of it.

156

When all the chests were in, Villa beckoned his men, one after the other, until about a dozen of them had come in and lined the walls. Then he came in himself. Pedro had retired to the bedroom and so had Chance.

For the first time, Villa saw the open chest and the spread-out notes. Through his own interpreter, he said, 'So you know?'

'We know. But what the hell, this money is good in Chihuahua, isn't it?'

The interpreter translated and a slightly puzzled expression came to Villa's heavy face. He nodded. 'It is good. The people have been ordered to turn in all of the old money on penalty of imprisonment.'

Dillman said, looking sour and angry, 'This wasn't what we agreed on, but if it's what you've brought, we'll take it. Maybe a vacation in Mexico wouldn't be so bad.'

Villa said bluntly, 'You know I meant to kill you before I left, don't you?'

Dillman pretended surprise. 'Kill us? Why?'

'So that you would not send the U.S. Army after us. We have twenty miles to go by road. It is only three or four miles across the mountains to Fort Bliss.'

Dillman said, 'I'll admit I was pretty goddam mad when I saw all this phony money of yours. Then I realized that it was good in Mexico as long as Pancho Villa is in control. And I figure that's going to be a long, long time.'

Dillman was talking for his life and for the lives of the others who had come with him. He tried to sound unconcerned but he didn't quite bring it off.

Villa said, again with his words being repeated through the interpreter, 'You say that now. But after we have gone, how do I know you will not go to the Army at Fort Bliss?'

'Why the hell would I lie to you?'

'Because you know that I intended to kill you all before I left. I am fighting for Mexico, señor, and I will take no chances I do not have to take.'

To the men standing along both walls, he issued a harsh command. Their guns came up. He said, 'Your guns, señores. All of them. Lay them carefully in a pile near the door.'

Angrily Dillman said, 'Damn it, I told you we'd take the money.'

Inflexibly, Villa said, 'You first, señor.'

Dillman glowered a moment. He stared into the bores of the Villista guns on both sides of the room. Then, with a fatalistic shrug, he crossed the room to the door and laid both his rifle and his revolver on the floor beside the door. Chance, watching from the bedroom, saw in Dillman's face that he no longer had any hope. He had resigned himself to death.

Villa pointed at a second man and this one, too, crossed the room and laid down his guns. So did a third, a fourth, a fifth, until the guns of all eight lay in a pile beside the door. Villa ordered that they be carried out, and half a dozen of his men carried out his command.

Dillman and his seven companions were now helpless. But Sam was not. He still had his revolver, and he was in the bedroom, out of sight, apparently forgotten for the time being by the Villistas.

Sam would have liked to save Dillman and his men if it had been possible. But he knew that it was not. They were about to pay the penalty they had accepted as possible when they made the deal with Villa to sell the guns to him.

Chance's first consideration, now, was for Lily, Jimmy, Pedro, and himself. And for this short span of time, all four seemed to have been forgotten by Villa in the tension of disarming Dillman and his men.

When the last of the weapons had been removed from the house, Villa went outside, leaving his remaining six men along the walls with their guns pointing at Dillman and his men. Chance could hear Villa shouting in Spanish, without understanding what was being said. But shortly the two machine gun wagons positioned at the sides of the house moved, jockeying themselves around until they formed a line with the other wagon, their machine gun pointing directly at the door.

Sam knew it was going to be an execution. Dillman and his men, Sam, Lily, Jimmy, and Pedro were all going to be lined up in front of the house. The three machine guns would open up, in a minute or less killing everybody standing in front of the house.

He knew that now was the only chance he was going to get. Villa was preoccupied with placing the guns and readying the execution. The Villistas inside the kitchen were preoccupied with watching Dillman and his men.

But at any instant, somebody was going to remember Chance, Pedro, Lily, and her son. After that there would be no opportunity to escape.

He couldn't save Dillman and his men, but maybe he could save Lily and her son. Whispering, he said, 'To the window! Quick!'

He pushed Lily so hard she staggered and almost fell. He himself gathered the still unconscious Jimmy in his arms. Pedro followed Lily to the window. He opened it, jumped up, and squeezed himself through the small opening, disappearing almost instantly as he dropped to the ground outside.

Sam handed Jimmy through next, knowing Lily wouldn't go while Jimmy remained behind. Pedro took him and laid him on the ground.

Lily went next, awkwardly because of her long skirt, but Pedro caught her too and put her down. And now Sam climbed to the window, eased himself through, and dropped to the ground outside.

No sooner did he plant his feet solidly on it than a shot rang out. Sam put out a hand, rough because of the urgency, and pushed Lily to the ground. Drawing his revolver, he turned in the direction from which the shot had come. He saw a Villista, not twenty feet away, and fired immediately before the man could get off a second shot.

The Mexican went down, dead before he hit the ground. Sam knew the shots would bring dozens of Villistas hurrying to this spot. He said, 'Come on! Quickly!'

Lily gathered up Jimmy's still-limp body in her arms and ran for the cover of the brushy creek bottom. Sam started to follow, just then noticing that Pedro lay curled up on the ground. He cursed, 'Damn!' and risked the time to kneel beside Pedro's motionless form. There was no movement in Pedro's chest and Sam knew that he was dead.

Straightening, he caught a glimpse of a man in the window above his head. The man had been drawn by the sounds of gunfire and in another instant, a dozen men would be around here shooting at him.

To Lily he yelled, 'Behind the icehouse! Quick!' He himself fired twice through the bedroom window and saw the Mexican soldier disappear. He didn't know whether he had hit the man or not and he didn't care. He was already sprinting toward the adobe icehouse, behind which Lily and her unconscious son were just now disappearing.

Behind him, more Villistas began firing from the bedroom window. Others appeared at the side of the house. Bullets kicked up geysers of dirt beside and ahead of Sam, and he dodged back and forth like a running jack rabbit, trying to keep one of them from getting a steady bead on him.

He felt one bullet twitch his hat, felt another sear his ribs. A third tore through his revolver holster, ripping it to shreds.

Ten feet short of the icehouse, with at least a dozen men now shooting at him, he left his feet and made a long, running dive. He hit the ground sliding, catching his would-be killers unawares. Their bullets buzzed harmlessly above him as he slid to the edge of the icehouse, came to hands and knees, and frantically crawled the rest of the way. No sooner had he disappeared, than one of the machine guns opened fire. Its wagon had been backed up until it commanded a view of the icehouse. The gun chattered, and its bullets thudded into the thick, adobe walls of the icehouse. They chewed at the wooden ceiling beams and kicked up geysers of dirt from the sod roof of the small building.

The firing stopped suddenly and Sam knew that now the Villistas were running toward the icehouse and that as soon as they appeared at its corners he, and Lily, and Jimmy were going to be dead. He poked his head around the corner, saw three Mexicans running toward him, and fired the last three rounds in his gun. Two of the men went down and the third turned and ran for the house.

As rapidly as he could, Sam ejected the empties from his gun, filled the cylinder from his belt, and scrambled to the other corner of the small icehouse. Two more Villistas were coming on this side, closer than the other three had been, in fact only a dozen feet away. Sam fired twice, rapidly, accurately. Both Mexicans went down.

Lily had her back to the adobe wall, Jimmy in her arms. She was terrified; that showed in her face. But she was watching Sam as if she had never doubted his ability to save her and her son.

He wryly hoped he could be worthy of her confidence as he poked his head around the other building corner. He saw no Villistas trying to rush the place. Instead he was greeted by a burst of machine gun fire that tore great chunks of adobe from the corner of the building, filled his eyes with dirt, but miraculously missed hitting him.

He pulled back. They couldn't stay here. For the moment the place was well covered by the machine gun but it was only a short matter of time before Villa realized he couldn't settle for a stalemate. Like Dillman and those with him, Sam Chance, Lily, and the boy had to die. Which meant he would execute a flanking movement until Sam, Lily, and Jimmy were in a crossfire from both sides.

He said, 'We've got to get out of here, and now. Villa will send men out to both sides in a minute and after that we won't have a chance.'

'What about that machine gun?'

'I don't know whether the gunner will be able to see us or not but it's a chance we've got to take. We can keep the icehouse between us and the gunner most of the way but there's a chance he'll spot us before we get to the creek.'

For an instant her eyes met his, still frightened, but with complete faith. He said, 'You go ahead. Don't hurry and don't run. See that twisted tree growing up out of the creek bottom? Head for that. I'll carry Jimmy and I'll be right behind.'

He didn't know how much protection he could give Lily and Jimmy by positioning his own body between them and the gun. But maybe some. Maybe some.

Lily started out, hurrying but not running. Sam, holding Jimmy against his chest, keeping his gun in his right hand, followed close behind.

All was quiet except for a lot of yelling in Spanish back at the house. It wasn't far to the cover provided by the cutbank that marked the edge of the creek bottom. But it seemed like miles.

They were halfway there. Then three quarters of the way. Sam turned his head and glanced back. He could see the head of the gunner on the wagon seat but he could not yet see the gun. The man was yelling something, and Sam knew the gunner had seen him.

To Lily he said, 'Crouch down and run. Dive into the creek bottom when you get there. I'll be right behind.'

She obeyed without question. She disappeared ahead of him. He was about to dive after her when the machine gun began chattering.

Most of the bullets went into the icehouse. One thudded into the trunk of the twisted tree. But by then Sam and Jimmy and Lily were safe for the moment. They were, at least, hidden from the gunner's sight. And hidden from the other Villistas, who also had begun shooting at them.

But there wasn't time to rest, because already the Villistas were running this way. Sam said, 'Come on! Follow me!' and set off through the underbrush as fast as he could run.

CHAPTER NINETEEN

Dillman was aware that Sam Chance, Pedro, Lily, and the unconscious boy had disappeared into the bedroom, even if the Villistas were not. The Mexicans were too busy disarming him and his men to have missed them immediately.

165

Dillman knew that, barring a miracle, he was going to die. He could see no escape from it. It wasn't any easier for him to contemplate death than it was for other men, but Dillman had been risking his life for too many years to have doubted that sooner or later it all had to come to an end. Now he made up his mind that if any of the Villistas missed the sheriff, the woman, the boy, and the Mexican cowboy, he was going to create a diversion. He'd kick up such a fuss that, for a few moments at least, the soldiers would forget about the others in the effort to subdue him.

No one missed the sheriff and the others though, and apparently they made an effort to escape through the back bedroom window, as a shot rang out, then another, and then all was still again.

One of Villa's men in the kitchen ran past Dillman trying to get into the bedroom. Dillman stuck out a foot and tripped him and the man went sprawling. But another was right behind. This one reached the window, stuck head and gun out and began firing.

A couple of shots from outside caught him squarely in the chest, driving him back. He sprawled on the bedroom floor, dead, blood soaking the front of his limp cotton shirt.

But Dillman didn't see this. He was in motion, diving for the man he had tripped, now sprawled on the floor and trying to get up. He was bigger than the Mexican, and stronger, but the Mexican was wiry and tough and he squirmed momentarily free of Dillman's grasp, rolled and brought his rifle savagely against Dillman's shoulder, numbing it.

Yet even with one arm nearly disabled from the blow, Dillman got his hands on the rifle and wrenched it away. Savagely and without mercy he brought its stock slamming against the Mexican's head. The soldier slumped.

Triggered by Dillman's action his seven men rushed the remaining four guards and overpowered them without a shot being fired. Quickly, they took away their weapons, tied them up, and made them lie down on the kitchen floor.

Holding the captured rifle, Dillman scrambled to his feet. Seeing that they were in control of the kitchen, Dillman glanced into the bedroom and found the other soldier dead on the floor. He turned, tossed the rifle to Phil Hibbert, then strode into the bedroom, and grabbed the dead Mexican's rifle.

He stripped both ammunition belts from the dead Mexican and withdrew the man's revolver from its holster. It was an old one, cap and ball, but it was loaded and held five shots.

The soldier from whom he had taken the first rifle had no revolver but he did have a belt pouch containing cartridges for the rifle, a single-shot Springfield. Dillman stooped, unbuckled the belt, and took it off.

There was now more shooting outside. One

of the machine guns opened up, chattering away until the belt of ammunition was gone. A few moments of quiet followed, then the gun gave a few short bursts to check out the new belt that had been inserted into it.

More silence. Then another burst from the machine gun that lasted only a few seconds and then stopped.

Dillman gave the revolver to Gwin. Ernst asked with a shaking voice, 'What are you going to do?'

'Put up a scrap. What the hell do you think we're going to do?'

'We'll all be killed!'

'You stupid bastard, what do you think is going to happen to us if we don't put up a scrap?'

'He might not kill us. We're American citizens.'

That was too ridiculous to answer. Dillman looked at Hibbert and at Gwin. 'Let's go. Right now they're busy with that woman and her kid. We'll never get a better chance.'

Chuck Hite asked, 'What about us? What do you want us to do?'

'Come out right behind us. We'll try to get those goddam machine gunners. Those without guns try to arm yourselves.' He started for the door, thinking that the sheriff, Lily MacDonald, her son, and the Mexican cowhand had either all gotten away or had all been killed.

There was a lot of angry shouting in the yard. Dillman didn't know much Spanish but he knew enough to know that some, if not all, of the fugitives had miraculously managed to escape.

Dillman paused at the door. The yelling continued in the yard, dominated by Villa's roaring, infuriated voice, ordering the Indian tracker and a number of men to get on the trail of the fugitives before they all got away in the growing darkness. Moments later, hoofbeats thundered outside the house, gradually fading as the pursuers put distance between them and the ranch.

Dillman knew he'd never have a better time than now. There was confusion in the yard. Many of the Villistas had ridden away in pursuit of the fugitives.

He could feel the close presence of Hibbert and Gwin beside him. He said, 'I'm going to try and get one of those machine guns. You two try and cover me.'

He didn't have to wait for their agreement. Both men were solid and dependable. He could hear Ernst still protesting fearfully as he flung open the door and plunged outside.

The machine gunners stared briefly in surprise, then tried to swing their guns. Helder, Hite, de la Torre, and Leon, scattered to right and left, firing on the run. Ernst stood like a fool in the doorway, arms raised as a signal that he wanted to surrender.

He was riddled by a burst from one of the machine guns. But by the time the sounds had died away, Dillman was beside the first wagon, the one on the left. He raised his rifle and shot the gunner in the chest. Then, flinging the rifle to the floorboards, he leaped up to the wagon seat.

He swung the gun toward the other two machine gunners who had been distracted by the gunfire from Hibbert and Gwin, positioned at the windows flanking the kitchen door, and riddled both Mexicans with a single burst.

Out of the corner of his eye he could see his other men scattering. Villa himself sat motionless on his horse for an instant, staring at what was happening with startled disbelief. Dillman swung the machine gun toward him, and Villa left his horse with surprising agility for a man so big. He dived behind the ammunition wagon. Dillman's next burst caught his horse, and the animal went to the ground, dead before he struck.

Knowing Villa was the key to all of this, Dillman now turned the machine gun on the ammunition wagon. He didn't know whether a wagonload of cartridges would explode in a kind of chain reaction if he fired a burst of machine gun bullets into it, but he was willing to give it a try.

As the gun muzzle centered on the ammunition wagon, he could see, out of the corner of his eye, Gwin and Hibbert dash out

170

of the house and climb to the wagon seats where the other machine guns were. For an instant he thought, 'Hell, we brought it off! We took 'em completely by surprise!'

Then his gun was chattering, the bullets tearing into the ammunition boxes loaded on the wagon behind which Villa had taken cover.

But even as they did, Villa appeared from behind the ammunition wagon, running like a man half his weight for the cover of one of the wagons that contained the crates of guns.

He was halfway there when the ammunition on the wagon began to explode. It started with a crackling of individual cartridges, exploded by the bullets from Dillman's machine gun. But with each cartridge that exploded, more exploded, and at last the whole thing went up in a final, gigantic explosion that blew the wagon apart, killed all four mules that were hitched to it, and left smoldering debris on the ground for a radius of a hundred yards.

Dillman took an instant for a lightning glance around, toward the cabin, toward the wagon behind which Villa had taken cover. Ernst lay dead in the doorway of the house, riddled by a score of bullets from the machine gun. Gwin and Hibbert were still manning the other two machine guns. Helder was dead, having failed to reach the dead Mexican from whom he had hoped to seize a gun.

De la Torre had a pistol and was standing at the corner of the cabin looking for something

171

at which to shoot. Hite was writhing on the ground, wounded, and Rogelio Leon was dead.

Heavy losses, Dillman thought, but better than what had been in store for them had they not put up a fight.

Suddenly from behind one of the ranch buildings, a Mexican soldier appeared, riding at a hard gallop, trailing a riderless horse. He managed to get behind the wagon where Villa was before Dillman could swing his gun. An instant later, the Mexican soldier and Villa appeared, galloping their horses directly away from the wagon, trying to keep it between them and the deadly fire of the machine guns until they would be out of range.

Dillman swung his gun and his finger tightened on the trigger. He knew he ought to kill Villa, but somehow or other his finger wouldn't tighten enough to make the gun fire. The others couldn't seem to bring their guns to bear. Villa and his rescuer galloped out of range.

Dillman didn't understand his own reluctance to kill the Mexican revolutionary. He knew Villa was a butcher. He knew Villa would have killed him and all his men if he could. He knew Villa had betrayed him with worthless money with which he hoped to pay for the guns.

But somehow he also knew that for all Villa's cruelties, he was a great man and a patriot. He was glad he had held his fire, even if it turned out disastrously for him in the end.

Right now, he and his men held control of the situation. They had the money, worthless as it was. They had the guns. They had destroyed the ammunition wagon and had forced Villa and his men to flee.

He also realized that, in control or not, their position was precarious. Snipers could kill the men manning the machine guns. They could not remain in control. Villa had too many men.

He roared at de la Torre, 'See if there's any coal oil in the house!'

Juan disappeared into the house. Dillman climbed down from the wagons. He didn't know whether the wagons containing the crated guns would burn or not but he intended to try. He was damned if he was going to let Villa get good guns in exchange for worthless money if it could be helped.

He did know there was a better chance of their burning if their contents were scattered, the crates broken open so that the fire could get a good draft as it burned. Furthermore, the grease with which the guns were smeared to protect them from rust would probably burn once it got a start.

He flung the canvas back and yanked one of the crates from a wagon bed. It fell to the ground, smashing as it did. Rifles spilled from the box, scattering. And Dillman stared in disbelief.

Suddenly he began to laugh. What he saw wasn't funny and he didn't really know why he laughed. The few rifles on the top layer in the boxes were complete and operable. Those below were missing their bolts, without which they were only so much iron and wood.

It was the irony, he supposed, that made him laugh. He glanced toward the riddled body of Ernst, wondering if he had known. Probably not. The bolts had probably been removed by an alert ordnance officer in charge of the U.S. Army arsenal, in case the guns should be stolen.

Dillman continued to laugh, while his men stared at him as if he had lost his mind. The irony of this was incomparable, Dillman thought. Worthless guns for worthless money. Good guns in the top layer of each crate in exchange for good money on the outside of each worthless package of currency.

And how many men had died for this charade? Dillman's laugh died on his lips. Too many and all uselessly.

Gone were all their dreams of being rich. Gone were Villa's dreams of modern rifles with which to lead his armies into the interior of Mexico.

De la Torre came from the house, carrying a can of coal oil with a potato stuck over its spout. Dillman said, 'Douse these wagons with it. Turn the mules loose. Then set the whole stinking mess afire. If you've got enough left, burn that damned useless money in the house too. Or upset the stove.'

He didn't really have anything against Lily MacDonald to make him burn her house. But he was angry now and feeling mean. Too much had gone into this to have it turn into a grisly joke.

Sniper fire now began coming from the creek banks and from behind the other ranch buildings. Dillman yelled, 'Stay under cover as much as you can! Boys, we may not be rich but we're going to get ourselves out of this!'

Del la Torre, after firing the wagons, went into the house and overturned the stove. He came out with the good U.S. yellowbacks in his hands.

Dillman knew that seeing the wagons burning would drive Villa to action, however reckless it might be. He roared, 'Get horses. We need four. Then let's get the hell out of here!'

He climbed back to the wagon seat and manned the machine gun while de la Torre went to the corral for horses. Dillman watched while he saddled them. Only when de la Torre had brought a horse did he climb down from the wagon seat and mount.

They were armed and alive. They had, perhaps, a thousand dollars between them in U.S. yellowbacks.

All of life's endeavors did not turn out right. This one had not. But at least, Dillman thought, he was still alive. He would live to fight another day.

Ernst, Helder, and Rogelio Leon were dead. Hite was shot in the chest and could not be loaded onto a horse without it killing him. That left Dillman himself, Jake Gwin, Hibbert, and Juan de la Torre.

From the ground, Chuck Hite called weakly, 'Dillman! For God's sake, don't leave me here!'

Dillman rode to him. Cartridges were still exploding like firecrackers from the heat of the smoldering pieces of the ammunition wagon. The guns were not burning, the coal oil having burned itself out, leaving only crates and parts of the wagons smoldering.

Dillman said, 'Chuck, you're shot in the chest. You wouldn't last half a mile on a horse, but if you stay here that woman will probably look after you as soon as Villa's gone.'

Hite looked at him longingly, but he apparently accepted the truth of what Dillman had said. Dillman hated leaving him, but he hadn't any choice. Already sniper bullets were kicking up dust all around him and the other three.

He whirled his horse and sank spurs into his sides. The others thundered after him. One horse, the one de la Torre was riding, had his rump grazed by a bullet and began to buck. De la Torre got him quickly under control.

Dillman felt empty and disappointed and

176

about half sick. The only thing he had to console himself with was that he was still alive.

Behind the four, Hite raised up on an elbow to watch them leave. His face suddenly twisted with excruciating pain. He fell back. His face composed itself and his chest was still.

CHAPTER TWENTY

Pancho Villa had little time for thought after Dillman and his men burst from the door of the house. Busy directing the pursuit of Sam Chance, the woman and child, and the Mexican cowhand, he had, at first, failed to pay enough attention to Dillman to know he had somehow overcome the guards inside the house and armed himself.

When Dillman reached the machine gun, however, Villa forgot everything but the pressing need to reach some kind of cover before the muzzle of that gun trained itself on him.

He dived from his horse toward the shelter of the ammunition wagon. He had no more than hit the ground, rolling, than the chatter of the gun began, the bullets tearing into the wagon's load. Bullets began popping as the machine gun bullets struck their caps, and it was like a chain reaction. The more bullets that discharged, the more that were discharged. In an instant, Villa knew, the whole wagon was going to go up in a huge explosion that would scatter red-hot, jagged cartridge cases like canister, killing everything within thirty or forty feet. He had to get away.

Risking the machine gun bullets, he got to his feet and sprinted for the cover of the nearest wagon containing guns, maybe thirty or forty feet away. He expected at any instant to be knocked from his feet and he dove for the shelter of the wagon, sliding the last few feet.

He was out of breath and dusty, but for the moment he was safe. And he was more furious than he could remember being in a long, long time. What was to have been a simple gun purchase had turned into a fiasco. The ammunition for the guns was gone and that was serious, but ammunition could be bought in El Paso for a price. The main thing now was to get the guns. That meant overpowering Dillman and his men, no easy task since they had control of all three machine guns. The ammunition wagon had, while Villa dived and skidded into the doubtful shelter of a wagonload of guns, finally exploded completely and red-hot pieces of jagged brass cartridge cases filled the air like rain. One cut Villa's cheek, and he raised a hand absently to brush away the blood.

From his prone position he heard rumbling in the ground beneath his head, the sound of hoofs galloping. He raised his head in time to see one of his men riding around the corner of the house at a dead run, trailing a riderless horse behind, holding one rein, the other being looped around the saddle horn.

Villa got to his hands and knees. A horseman if nothing else, he was running at top speed as the rider passed him and he was ready when the man handed him the rein. He flung himself to the horse's back, digging spurs deep, laying low over the horse's withers so as to present a smaller target for the machine gunners.

Again he kept waiting for a bullet to smash into his back. But, strangely, the gun was silent. He turned his head, startled and amazed to see the machine gun with its muzzle trained on him but silent, not firing.

It was something he did not understand, unless the gunner was out of amunition. Yet he knew that could not be it because he saw a half-used belt hanging from the gun.

Mercy, restraint, failure to kill one's enemies were things Pancho Villa did not understand. But he had no time now to puzzle over it. Galloping, he was soon out of range, able to halt his horse, turn and stare back at what was happening.

He saw Dillman yank back the canvas from one of the wagons loaded with guns. He pulled one of the crates from it, letting it smash upon the ground. The contents spilled out. And now the strangest thing of all occurred. Dillman, after staring at the rifles on the ground a moment, began unexpectedly to laugh.

Thoroughly puzzled, Villa roared at his men to begin firing. From the cover of the brush-lined creek, they began firing at Dillman and his men. But distance was great, their guns old, and in many cases so rusted were their bores that they didn't hit anything.

Unable to understand what was happening at the house, but acutely aware that things were rapidly getting out of hand, Villa retreated to the cover of the stream bed, where perhaps forty of his men were bunched, awaiting orders from him.

Villa watched with disbelief while Dillman and his men doused the wagons with coal oil and set them afire. One of Dillman's men went into the house and emerged almost at once. Smoke began to pour from the door of the house.

Still puzzling to Villa was the way Dillman had laughed as he looked at the spilled rifles from the broken case. To Lieutenant Mora he said, 'Watch them. When they leave go after them. I don't want anyone left alive who can get word to the soldiers at Fort Bliss.'

Mora saluted. '*Sí, mi general.*'

The mules were loose, having been released by Dillman's men before they tried firing the wagons with the small amount of coal oil they had available. Villa said, 'Have some of the men catch those mules. We will need them.'

He watched for a moment more. The fires briefly flared, then died as soon as the coal oil was gone, leaving only smoldering corners of wagon beds, gun cases, and canvas covers. The guns, he thought, would be intact even if the ammunition was gone.

He turned his horse and, accompanied by four soldiers, rode along the creek bed following the trail left by the Tarahumara and his dozen men.

* * *

Sam ran tirelessly through the scrub brush and stunted trees in the bottom of the creek. He was carrying the still-unconscious Jimmy, whose weight was negligible in his arms. Ahead of him ran Lily, trying her best, but hampered by her skirts and rapidly growing short of breath. She halted briefly, partly to pull her skirts up above her knees so that they would not slow her down, partly to catch her breath.

She looked at Sam, face flushed, eyes terrified. He could see that she was trying hard to maintain her faith in him but that she was thoroughly scared.

Sam knew that if the three of them stayed together they didn't have a chance. As he hesitated, he heard the chatter of the machine guns back at the house. For an instant he thought it was the execution of Dillman and his men. But the gun was silent a moment, then chattered again as a new belt was inserted into it.

Frowning, he waited for other sounds and was rewarded by the muffled popping faintly heard over the chatter of the machine gun, popping that increased, sounding like strings of firecrackers, and finally by the explosion of the ammunition wagon as it blew up and scattered red-hot parts of cartridges in all directions.

He said, 'That had to have been the ammunition wagon. And if it went up, it's got to mean that somehow Dillman and his friends have gotten hold of the machine guns. Probably while Villa was busy worrying about us.'

Gone might be the wagonload of ammunition. But the wagons loaded with guns remained and Villa would be taking them to Mexico as soon as he got rid of Dillman and his men. That meant he still didn't dare leave anyone alive to send the U.S. Army after him.

Sam glanced around. He said, 'Without horses, you haven't got a chance of keeping up. Is there anyplace you can hide?'

Lily said, 'There's a cave in the riverbank where Jimmy sometimes plays. It's small, but maybe we can pull some brush over the front of it.'

'Where is it?'

She pointed. 'Over there.'

'How far?'

'Not very far.'

Sam looked at the ground. He knew his time was running out. He also knew that when the Villistas came after him, the Tarahumara scout would probably be guiding them.

The ground here was covered with leaves. He handed Jimmy to Lily. 'Go there and hide. Try to pull brush over the entrance if you can. Don't come out until I come for you. All right?'

She nodded, the complete trust back in her eyes, nearly overshadowing her fear. Carrying Jimmy, she hurried away, at right angles to the direction they had been traveling. Sam waited until she was out of sight. Then, carefully, he picked up a dead branch and ever so meticulously, tried to obliterate her footprints for at least half a dozen feet. He knew the Tarahumara would read the prints where they had stopped while Lily caught her breath. So when he went on, he brought each foot down hard with every step so that it would appear he had picked Lily up and was carrying her, as well as the boy. He hoped that by the time the Tarahumara realized he had made a mistake, the place where Lily had left the trail would be trampled by the soldiers accompanying the scout and be undecipherable.

Already he could hear them coming, crashing through the brush. He ran, deliberately slamming each foot down doubly hard to maintain the illusion that he was carrying a heavy weight.

Running, he tried to puzzle out what had happened back at the house. Perhaps Dillman had momentarily obtained the upper hand. But Chance knew it couldn't last. Dillman had only seven men. Villa had nearly seventy.

And now he alone was pitted against at least a score of those seventy men. And he didn't even have a horse.

He had little chance of coming out alive. All he could hope was that Villa, pressed for time, would leave before finding Lily and her son. It was late in the afternoon and would soon be dark. Villa would want to leave for Mexico as soon as it got dark, even if he had to risk leaving some of the gringos alive behind. He would probably realize that getting rid of their horses, their means of transport, would be just as effective as getting rid of them.

Time, then, was what Sam needed to survive. And to obtain that time he had to have a horse. His own was safely tied a long ways upstream, beyond his reach.

Ambush was the answer, risky as it was. He had no idea exactly how many Villistas would be with the Tarahumara scout. But maybe, if he could shoot one man out of the saddle, the others would take cover, if only momentarily. That might give Sam a chance to get a horse.

Still running, he passed an unusually thick clump of brush, over which a scrub tree had grown. He halted, crouched behind it, and discovered that he could see through it but that

184

it was unlikely he would be spotted right away since the brush clump was a dozen yards to one side of the trail.

The danger was that his revolver bullet might be deflected by a branch, and if that happened he'd never get a chance for a second shot.

Crouching now, breathing hard, he waited for them to catch up with him. He poked his revolver as far through the brush as he dared, and even broke a couple of branches that were in the way. He held his breath a moment and then, realizing he was doing so, let it sigh slowly out.

Never in Sam's life had he faced such odds. He heard the crashing of brush made by the pursuit growing closer and felt vastly relieved that they had, at least, passed the place where Lily had taken Jimmy and headed for the cave without seeing it.

Then he saw the scout, riding at a trot, eyes on the ground. Behind him came a dozen of Villa's soldiers in their nondescript uniforms. They seemed only half alert, relying, no doubt, upon the scout to warn them of the nearness of their prey.

Chance knew he ought to let them go by and take the one in the rear. He also knew he didn't dare. The Tarahumara was too damned good and he'd pick up immediately where Sam had left the trail. Sam wished belatedly that he'd had the foresight to go on a hundred yards and then come back to his hiding place. But he hadn't and now it was too late.

Steadying his gun, he fired, at the neck of the Tarahumara's horse. The animal fell as if he had been clubbed. The Indian was thrown sprawling on the ground.

Before he had time to comprehend what was happening, Sam shot the rider immediately behind him. The man tumbled from the saddle and the horse, frightened, ran forward for perhaps half a dozen yards.

The soldiers were scattering, some leaving their mounts, some reining them aside. Sam was up and running almost before the echo of his second shot had died away. The dead soldier's horse was now perhaps a dozen yards ahead of where the Tarahumara lay on the ground. Running, Sam vaulted to the saddle, afterward leaning forward and gathering up the reins. He sank his spurs into the horse's sides as the scout and the soldiers, realizing what had happened, raised up and began firing.

They were excited and taken by surprise and their aim was wild. Sam spurred the Mexican horse, gaining several hundred yards before the Tarahumara and the Mexicans regained their composure, mounted, and took up the pursuit.

He had mobility now but he was a long ways from being in the clear. He couldn't outrun them all. But he might stay ahead of them until it got dark. Failing that, he would have to lay another ambush, hoping that heavy losses would make them abandon the chase.

CHAPTER TWENTY-ONE

It was risky galloping a horse so recklessly through this brushy creek bottom where snags and downed trees lay across his path and ground squirrel holes were hazards his horse could not see and therefore could not avoid.

Sam leaned low over his horse's withers. He didn't know how many bullets remained in his gun but he thought he had only one. He drew the gun, spun the cylinder, and discovered that he was right.

Holding the reins and gun in his left hand, he awkwardly withdrew cartridges from his belt one by one and reloaded the gun. The crashing and shouting behind him told him the Tarahumara and the Mexicans were at least keeping pace.

Reining to the right, he came out of the brush and into the flat, sandy bed of the near-dry stream. The neck of his horse was lathering and the animal was breathing hard.

In the west, the sun was down, but it cast a golden glow upon the clouds above the horizon, a glow that would last ten or fifteen minutes at least.

Sam wondered about Lily and her son. He hoped they were all right. He hoped they had reached the cave and that they would remain there, quiet and still, until he came for them.

The Tarahumara and the Mexicans, following his trail, now also came out of the brush and into the open, sandy bottom of the stream. A few of the Mexicans spread out to right and left and began firing. None of the bullets came close, the nearest kicking up a geyser of sand half a dozen yards to Sam's right.

But they were gaining on him, a fact he couldn't understand. His horse should have been able to stay ahead unless he had been ridden harder than the others had. He remembered the troops that had been sent after Pew and his unsavory crew and supposed the former owner of this horse might have been one of them.

Desperately he glanced toward the west. They were going to overtake him before the light faded from the sky. Dark wouldn't save him. He'd have to think of something else that would.

The creek took a sharp bend and for the briefest instant, Sam was hidden from the view of those pursuing him. So suddenly that his horse nearly fell, he reined him hard over, spurred him savagely up the cutbank and into the brush at the side of the stream.

He was off the horse instantly, dropping the

reins, letting the horse run on for fifteen or twenty feet. He held his breath, hoping the animal had been trained to stop when the reins were dragging, but he had no time to check. He flung himself prone, and as the Tarahumara came around the bend, raised his revolver, holding it with both hands and steadying it in the crotch of one of the branches of the brush clump behind which he lay. Once more he shot the Tarahumara's horse, for some reason reluctant to kill the man himself.

His second shot killed a second horse, his third sent the next horse in line to bucking so that his rider sailed off and landed on his back in the sand.

Three shots gone, two left. Sam got up and scrambled through the clawing brush toward his horse, standing trembling less than twenty feet away.

The shots and his crashing approach frightened the animal, and he trotted away from Sam. Sam cursed, glanced over his shoulder, then approached more slowly, speaking soothingly to the horse. If he couldn't catch the damned horse, he was trapped here and the Mexican soldiers wouldn't take long to recover from their surprise and come after him.

The horse's reins became caught in a clump of thorny brush long enough for Sam to reach the animal. He mounted and sank spurs and the horse galloped away again.

It had seemed only a couple of minutes, that

last ambush and confrontation, but it must have been a lot longer because now all the golden glow was gone from the western sky and dusk was creeping across the land. Sam kept his horse going, straight out of the creek bottom and up onto the prairie beyond. He couldn't see Lily's house from here but he could see what looked like a thin plume of smoke from the direction in which it lay. Wanting a better look, he spurred the weary horse up the nearest rise.

Out of the creek bottom came the Tarahumara, riding a horse commandeered from one of the Villistas, and a scattering of soldiers followed him. Oddly, he stopped just beyond the cutbank and the trees and brush and sat his horse staring up the slope at Sam.

Sam was out of rifle range, at least in this kind of light. Perhaps the Tarahumara knew he now had no chance to overtake Sam before darkness overtook them both. Or perhaps he was thinking that twice Sam could have killed him and had killed his horse instead.

Impassively he sat, staring up the hill. Sam looked back, understanding the Indian in that instant perhaps better than the Indian understood himself.

Silhouetted against the graying sky, Sam raised an arm in a silent salute. It was unacknowledged for so long that Sam thought perhaps his gesture had not been seen, or that the Indian's animosity was greater than he had thought it was. But at last the Indian's arm went up, briefly, and then dropped again. He turned his horse and disappeared into the brushy creek bottom, followed by the Mexican soldiers who remained.

Sam waited until it was fully dark. Then, avoiding the creek bottom, he headed back toward the cave where Lily and Jimmy were waiting for him to come.

*   *   *

Villa met the Tarahumara and the soldiers accompanying him half a mile from where the Tarahumara gave up the chase. 'Did you get them?'

The Tarahumara managed to show no fear although he knew how near to death he was for having failed. He shook his head. 'He escaped in the darkness, General. The woman and the boy are hidden somewhere between here and the house.'

It was, perhaps, well that he could not see the expression on Villa's face. There was a long silence, while the Tarahumara waited to see if Villa would draw his revolver and shoot him down. Apparently Villa decided he needed the tracker because he turned his horse and headed back toward the ranch.

Villa was not used to failure and it always infuriated him. He had come here expecting to acquire five thousand excellent repeating rifles

191

with ammunition for them. Now the ammunition was gone, the money, which for all its worthlessness in the United States, had value in Mexico and had cost a considerable amount to print, was burned, along with the small ranch house. And the rifles . . . well he still had the rifles if he could get them to Mexico. But he had double-crossed Dillman and the first thing Dillman would do if he got away would be to alert the Army at Fort Bliss. And if Dillman didn't get away, Sam Chance, sheriff of Cruces County, would alert the commandant at the fort.

But Villa had not become one of Mexico's foremost revolutionary generals by admitting failure easily. He still had more than forty men. He would take the rifles to Mexico, and if the U.S. Army intervened, then he would give them a battle they would not soon forget.

He reached the spot directly below the ranch house and rode his horse up out of the bed of the stream. He rode past the icehouse and the other buildings.

The house was gutted inside, but the fire was only smoldering in the roof. The money was gone, of course, thought Villa, but he turned his head and ordered a couple of his men to try and recover the money chests just in case some of the money was unburned.

He noticed that, while the mules had all been caught, they had not been hitched to the wagons that contained the crated rifles.

Lieutenant Mora was back from the pursuit of Dillman. In the faint glow coming from the house, he could see the narrowed eyes, the fury that was in Villa's face. Villa asked, 'You got them?'

Mora shook his head fearfully, like the Tarahumara expecting to be shot, 'They got away in the darkness, General.'

'Why are not the mules hitched to these wagons? Why are we not ready to leave?'

Mora's voice actually trembled. 'Look at the rifles, General.'

Villa swung ponderously from his horse and strode to where a couple of rifle cases lay smashed upon the ground. One of the soldiers had found a lantern and had lighted it. He brought it close so the general could see.

Villa saw first the complete rifles that had been on the top of each crate. Then he saw the ones that had been underneath, the ones without any bolts.

Villa was a man of violent temper and for several moments he looked as if he was going to explode. But he was also a man who could see the irony of this, and gradually the red faded from his face. The throbbing veins in his forehead subsided, the narrowness disappeared from his eyes.

Suddenly he began to laugh. He had tried to betray Dillman by bringing him worthless Mexican currency when the agreement had called for either gold or American currency.

But Dillman had betrayed him too, bringing useless rifles to guard himself against Villa's perfidy.

Mora and the others were staring at him, some tentatively smiling with him, others still trembling.

Villa roared, 'Get what good guns there are in each case. Each man is to carry as many as he can. We will take the route over the mountains so we needn't worry about the gringo soldiers from Fort Bliss.'

He watched while the other wagons were uncovered, their crates opened, and the workable rifles removed from them. He ordered the machine guns removed from the wagon seats where they had been bolted earlier. Each was loaded onto a separate horse that had belonged to one of Villa's casualties. The ammunition belts that remained were also loaded carefully.

Finally, when all the usable guns and ammunition were in the hands of his men, he led his remaining troops up out of the little valley and into the rough mountains that led to Mexico.

CHAPTER TWENTY-TWO

Sam Chance watched the Mexicans from the hilltop. It was now completely dark, but they

194

had found several lanterns and were using them to provide light for dismounting the machine guns, for selecting the rifles from the boxes that, Sam guessed, must be the only ones that were workable. Dillman had, apparently, brought crates of rifles that were somehow defective except for the layer on top. Otherwise, Villa would be taking them all to Mexico.

There was still some fire in the roof of the house, and this provided a certain amount of additional light.

Sam ached to go to Lily and Jimmy, who were still, he hoped, hiding safely in the cave. But he knew that before he did he ought to be sure the Villistas all had gone.

Lily's house was gutted. Her two Mexican cowhands were dead. The question of where they would live after they were married had apparently been solved for them.

He watched while the machine guns were dismounted and loaded on the extra horses that Villa now had because of the men he'd lost. He watched while the rifles were lashed together with rope and slung three or four on each side of some of the soldiers' saddles.

At last, when all was done, Villa led his troops out of the valley and into the mountains leading to Mexico.

No troops from Fort Bliss, even if Dillman alerted them, would be able to catch him now. And for some strange reason, Sam was glad.

Villa had tried to kill him, and would have if he'd been able to. But Sam doubted if he'd have killed Lily and her son. The gravest danger to them had come from Pew and his gang of unwashed cutthroats, all of whom now, fortunately, were dead.

He rode his horse down the hill as soon as the last of the Villistas had left the yard. He didn't know exactly where the cave was where Lily and Jimmy were hidden but he knew where he had left them and he figured they'd hear him if he called out to them.

He reached the deserted yard, his horse shying away both from the smell of smoke and that of blood. He rode straight beyond, down into the brushy creek bottom.

Lily would marry him now, he thought, perhaps as soon as tomorrow. Feeling a growing excitement he called, 'Lily! Jimmy! It's Sam! You can come out now!'

He heard nothing and for an instant felt the coldness of fear in his chest. Maybe they had been discovered by some of Villa's men. Maybe they were dead.

Frantically he roared, 'Lily! It's me! You can come out now!'

He heard what sounded like a faint cry and immediately turned his horse toward it. Recklessly, disregarding snags and downed trees, he spurred the animal toward the sound.

Near the cutbank he caught a blur of white and knew this had to be Lily. He was off his horse in an instant, running toward her. When he reached Lily, he caught her in his arms and held her so tightly that she could scarcely breathe. He felt a tug on his sleeve and, looking down, saw that Jimmy was standing there, demanding attention from him with his insistent tugging on his sleeve.

Sam released Lily and lifted Jimmy up. And now he held them both, while Lily wept nearly uncontrollably because the terror she had lived with so many long hours now was gone and she was safe.

The first thing Sam could say was, 'Is Jimmy all right? Are *you* all right?'

She nodded without speaking, her tear-wet cheek against his. He said, 'Then let's get to town. I'll send some men out here tomorrow to clean up this mess.' He held Jimmy's form easily with his left arm and, with his right around Lily's waist, led them back to where he had left his horse.

He helped her up, boosted Jimmy up in front of her, then he mounted behind the saddle. The slight wounds he had sustained were sore, but the bleeding had almost completely stopped.

He guided the horse upstream to the place where he had left his own horse earlier. Dismounting, he untied the animal and mounted him. Leading the horse with Lily and Jimmy riding it, he headed out toward town.

Lily was silent as the horse picked his way up out of the creek bed and crossed the yard to the

197

still-smoldering house. Sam said, 'Not much left inside. You want me to try getting anything out of there?'

She shook her head. 'There's nothing important enough in there to risk your getting burned.'

They passed the wagons still parked in the yard, some still smoldering. Sam dismounted and quickly glanced at the rifles scattered around to determine why Villa had rejected them. They had no bolts. He got back up on his horse.

Lily said, 'What happened? Why did he leave all those rifles here?'

'Most of them had no bolts so they weren't any more good to Villa than the worthless money he brought to pay for them was to Dillman and his bunch. Dillman got a few hundred dollars of good money, I suppose. And Villa got three machine guns and a few workable rifles. They both got more than they deserved.'

They rode away, taking the road toward town. Sam was puzzled by her silence and at last he said, 'You're quiet. Why? Everything is going to be all right.'

'I ... I have to tell you something, Sam, before we go any farther. I told Mike before I married him and I owe you as much.'

'You don't have to tell me anything.'

'Don't stop me, Sam. You have to know. One of those men, the one named Quigley, recognized me. Sooner or later someone else will too. I used to work in a saloon in San Antonio.' She waited for the silence, or worse, for the harsh words he might have to say.

He was neither silent, nor did he utter any harsh words. With almost total unconcern he said immediately, 'So what? I've known you over five years and I know all I need to know. Don't think you're going to get out of marrying me that easily.'

Lily felt the flood of warm tears come to her eyes, felt them run down across her cheeks. She asked in a voice that Sam could scarcely hear, 'Sam, can Jimmy and I ride with you?'

He halted his horse, swung down, reached up and lifted both her and Jimmy to the ground. Then he lifted them, one by one, to the back of his horse. He mounted behind them, the reins of the Mexican horse tied to the saddle horn.

Lily took his free arm in both her hands and pulled it around her waist. He brought her head forward, bent and kissed her on the cheek.

At last, she thought, the past was dead. Thinking of that, she missed what Sam whispered in her ear. She asked, 'What did you say?'

'I said tomorrow. Tomorrow afternoon. Can you get ready to be married tomorrow afternoon?'

Never again would Lily put something off

that she knew was right. She had nearly lost Sam today and she wasn't going to risk losing him again. She turned her face to him, smiling, and said, 'I'll be ready any time you say.'

This time, his lips found hers in spite of the dark. Jimmy was asleep by now. Sam's arm tightened around Lily and he touched his horse's sides lightly with his spurs, forcing him to trot. Damn it, they both had waited long enough.

Lewis B. Patten wrote more than ninety Western novels in thirty years and three of them won Golden Spur Awards from the Western Writers of America and the author himself the Golden Saddleman Award. Indeed, this points up the most remarkable aspect of his work: not that there is so much of it, but that so much of it is so fine. Patten was born in Denver, Colorado, and served in the U.S. Navy 1933–1937. He was educated at the University of Denver during the war years and became an auditor for the Colorado Department of Revenue during the 1940s. It was in this period that he began contributing significantly to Western pulp magazines, fiction that was from the beginning fresh and unique and revealed Patten's lifelong concern with the sociological and psychological affects of group psychology on the frontier. He became a professional writer at the time of his first novel, *MASSACRE AT WHITE RIVER* (1952). The dominant theme in much of his fiction is the notion of justice, and its opposite, injustice. In his first novel it has to do with exploitation of the Ute Indians, but as he matured as a writer he explored this theme with significant and poignant detail in small towns throughout the early West. Crimes, such as rape or lynching, were often at the center of his stories. When the values embodied in these small towns are examined closely, they are found to be wanting. Conformity is always easier than taking a stand. Yet, in Patten's view of the American West, there is usually a man or a woman who refuses to conform. Among his finest titles, always a difficult choice, surely are *A KILLING AT KIOWA* (1972), *RIDE A CROOKED TRAIL* (1976), and his many fine contributions to Doubleday's Double D series, including *VILLA'S RIFLES* (1977). *THE LAW AT COTTONWOOD* (1978), and *DEATH RIDES A BLACK HORSE* (1978).

We hope you have enjoyed this Large Print book. Other Chivers Press or Thorndike Press Large Print books are available at your library or directly from the publishers. For more information about current and forthcoming titles, please call or write, without obligation, to:

Chivers Press Limited
Windsor Bridge Road
Bath BA2 3AX
England
Tel. (0225) 335336

OR

Thorndike Press
P.O. Box 159
Thorndike, ME 04986
USA
Tel. (800) 223-6121
(207) 948-2962
(in Maine and Canada, call collect)

All our Large Print titles are designed for easy reading, and all our books are made to last.